# CHASING HER SCENT

# What Reviewers Say About
# MJ Williamz's Work

### Exposed

"The love affair between Randi and Eleanor goes along in fits and starts. It is a wonderful story, and the sex is hot. Definitely read it as soon as you have a chance!"—Janice Best, Librarian (Albion District Library)

### Shots Fired

"MJ Williamz, in her first romantic thriller, has done an impressive job of building the tension and suspense. Williamz has a firm grasp of keeping the reader guessing and quickly turning the pages to get to the bottom of the mystery. *Shots Fired* clearly shows the author's ability to spin an engaging tale and is sure to be just the beginning of great things to follow as the author matures."—*Lambda Literary Review*

"Williamz tells her story in the voices of Kyla, Echo, and Detective Pat Silverton. She does a great job with the twists and turns of the story, along with the secondary plot. The police procedure is first rate, as are the scenes between Kyla and Echo, as they try to keep their relationship alive through the stress and mistrust."
—*Just About Write*

### Scene of the Crime

"This story was so promising, the initial introduction and setup with highly intriguing and the plot held a lot of mystery. ...It was a nice story if you want a romance with an underlying theme that isn't too heavy or graphic. I really enjoyed the story and hope maybe there will be a future story for Cullen and Julia as there is more potential there for them now they have freedom to explore their relationship."—*LESBIreviewed*

## Forbidden Passions

"*Forbidden Passions* is 192 pages of bodice ripping antebellum erotica not so gently wrapped in the moistest, muskiest pantalets of lesbian horn dog high jinks ever written. While the book is joyfully and unabashedly smut, the love story is well written and the characters are multi-dimensional. ...*Forbidden Passions* is the very model of modern major erotica, but hidden within the sweet swells and trembling clefts of that erotica is a beautiful May–September romance between two wonderful and memorable characters."
—*Rainbow Reader*

## Sheltered Love

"The main pair in this story is astoundingly special, amazingly in sync nearly all the time, and perhaps the hottest twosome on a sexual front I have read to date. ...This book has an intensity plus an atypical yet delightful original set of characters that drew me in and made me care for most of them. Tantalizingly tempting!"
—*Rainbow Book Reviews*

## Speakeasy

"*Speakeasy* is a bit of a blast from the past. It takes place in Chicago when Prohibition was in full flower and Al Capone was a name to be feared. The really fascinating twist is a small speakeasy operation run by a woman. She was more than incredible. This was such great fun and I most assuredly recommend it. Even the bloody battling that went on fit with the times and certainly spiced things up!"
—*Rainbow Book Reviews*

**"In the Bell Tower" in Women of the Dark Streets**

"New Orleans and a sexy female vampire helps an awkward visitor blossom and make sweet, sweet love all night long. Delicious!"
—*Rainbow Book Reviews*

**Heartscapes**

"The development of the relationship was well told and believable. Now the sex actually means something and MJ Williamz certainly knows how to write a good sex scene. Just when you think life has finally become great again for Jesse, Odette has a stroke and can't remember her at all. It is heartbreaking. Odette was a lovely character and I thought she was well developed. She was just the right person at the right time for Jesse. It was an engaging book, a beautiful love story."—*Inked Rainbow Reads*

Visit us at www.boldstrokesbooks.com

# By the Author

# CHASING HER SCENT

*by*

## MJ Williamz

2025

# CHASING HER SCENT

ISBN 13: 978-1-63679-900-1

THIS TRADE PAPERBACK ORIGINAL IS PUBLISHED BY
BOLD STROKES BOOKS, INC.
P.O. BOX 249
VALLEY FALLS, NY 12185

FIRST EDITION: NOVEMBER 2025

CREDITS
EDITOR: CINDY CRESAP
PRODUCTION DESIGN: SUSAN RAMUNDO
COVER DESIGN BY TINA MICHELE

# Acknowledgments

First thanks go to my awesome beta readers, Sarah and Sue. A special thanks to Carrie and Kathy for their feedback and advice. And, of course, a huge thank you to the incomparable Tina Michele for her incredible artwork for the cover of this book.

I would be remiss if I didn't thank all the wonderful folks at Bold Strokes Books for their continued support over the past fifteen plus years. Thank you, Cindy, Stacia, Sandy, Rad, and all the rest.

## Dedication

For Laydin, my everything

# PROLOGUE

*France, 1789*

Margot and Josephine lay together on the hard bed in the dusty hovel. Margot's hefty breasts heaved as she struggled to catch her breath.

"You are beautiful," Josephine murmured. "I love the flush on your body. You look like a woman who has been loved right."

"You have a biased opinion," said Margot.

"Oui. But I can't get enough of you."

She kissed her way down Margot's voluptuous body until she came to rest between her legs. The scent of their recent lovemaking was strong, and she tasted Margot's pleasure as she tenderly licked her pink beauty.

"Again?" said Margot.

"Oui," said Josephine. "Always."

She pleased Margot with her mouth and her fingers, wishing she had more ways to show her how much she loved her. Their time together was so special and always so fleeting. Josephine knew she would have to dress and get back to court. Eventually. But not right then. Then, all that mattered was her lover's naked body and the way they made each other feel.

When Margot had cried out again, Josephine kissed her way back up until she reached her full, bruised lips so she could share Margot's special flavor with her.

As they kissed, Margot's fingers found Josephine's center and worked their magic until Josephine pleaded that she had nothing left.changed to

"When can we do this again? I don't want to wait days. I want to see you again tonight," said Margot.

"I will try to come back. But I must tend to Her Majesty. Things are very scary for her right now. I must be her strength."

"You are my strength, too, my Josephine. Please remember that."

"I never forget. Now, help me into my corset, please. I need to get to court."

Margot helped Josephine get dressed and kissed her one final time before letting her go.

"Come back soon," said Margot. "Please?"

"I shall do what I can."

Later that night, Josephine knocked on Margot's door. In her free hand, she held a small pouch containing something she couldn't wait to share with her.

Margot opened the door wearing a dressing gown.

"Have you not gotten dressed since this afternoon?" Josephine smiled.

"I didn't see the point. I'm so glad you came back. I've missed you."

She untied her gown and let it fall to the floor.

"Holy Mary, Mother of God. You take my breath away," said Josephine.

"Prove it."

Josephine kissed Margot hard on the mouth and walked her back to the bed. She eased her down on it and lay on top of her.

"Oh, no," said Margot. "You need to undress first."

"Help me."

Together, they got Josephine's layers off, with much kissing and suckling by Margot. They came together, naked, on the bed and kissed for an eternity. Hands roamed, fondled, and probed. They found release with each other as they'd never found before.

"I should go," said Josephine. "But first, I have a surprise for you."

"Another one? I'm worn out."

"No, mon amour. A different surprise. Before I give it to you, I must ask you to swear something."

"Why? Just give it to me."

"I need you to swear," repeated Josephine.

"You're worrying me."

"Swear you'll guard it with your life."

"Josephine... How can I swear that? What is so important even that I must?"

Josephine crossed the room to the small table and picked up the pouch.

"Swear, Margot."

"What's in the pouch?"

"Before I show you, you must swear you'll let no harm come to it."

"Why?" said Margot.

"You must. Do you swear?"

"Oui. Fine. I swear."

"Close your eyes, mon amour," said Josephine.

"Do I need to be scared?"

"Do you trust me?"

"Implicitly." Margot closed her eyes.

Josephine opened the pouch and took out a diamond tiara. She gently, carefully, placed in on Margot's head.

"Keep those eyes closed." She picked up the hand mirror and placed it in Margot's hand. "You may open them now."

Margot's hand flew to her mouth as she took in her reflection.

"Holy Virgin Mary. Where did you get this?"

"Where do you think?"

"It's not...*hers*, is it?"

"Oui. She doesn't want it lost, so I'm entrusting it in your care. When Her Majesty gets to Vienna, we'll return it to her somehow. For now, you look divine. Here's this as well."

Margot opened the locket. There was a portrait of the queen wearing the tiara.

"I need to ask you something," she said. She stared deep into Josephine's violet eyes.

"Anything."

"Are the rumors true?"

"What rumors might those be?" Though Josephine needn't have inquired. She knew.

"Are you and Marie lovers? Is that why she gave you these? So you'll have something to remember her by?"

"You're talking nonsense. You are my only lover, Margot. The only one I want or will ever need."

"Swear?"

"On anything and everything holy. Now, swear you'll protect these."

"Oh, my darling Josephine. I will indeed guard these with my life. You needn't worry."

"I knew I could trust you. Now, unfortunately, I must get home. I shall see you soon."

"I love you, Josephine."

"And I, you."

Josephine kissed Margot goodbye and let herself out into the evening.

## CHAPTER ONE

*Quebec City, 2024*

"Damn, it's a dreary day out there." Lisette shook out her umbrella before letting the door to the bookstore close behind her.

"Morning, boss. Coffee is just about brewed. Come on in and get warm."

Lisette Mouton noticed that Gabby had already lit a fire in the rustic stone fireplace. She was more grateful for her wonderful employee every day.

"That sounds wonderful. I think I'll sip some coffee and warm up in front of the fire before I start on the books."

"Reading or reconciling?" Gabby laughed.

"Now, Gabby. You know I'd love nothing more than to curl up in front of the fire with any one of these books. But owning a bookstore comes with responsibilities. Unfortunately. So, I'll be locked in my office, watching the rain pelt the windows, and reconciling yesterday's accounting. Then we need to talk about the bookfair in the square. It's only a few months away. Why don't you work up a flyer for us to distribute?"

"Yes, ma'am. I'll be happy to."

"I wish I had time to do it myself," said Lisette. "But you are such an artist. I know you won't disappoint. You can do it freehand or on the Mac. Either way is fine."

"You got it. What's the theme again?"

"The French Revolution."

"That'll be fun. I'm all over it."

"Enjoy. I'm taking my coffee to the fire now."

Lisette sipped the hot elixir and contemplated life. Approaching forty, she wasn't getting any younger. She was proud of the fact that she'd owned the bookstore, Librarie De Trésors, for seven years. It had been a dream of hers for as long as she could remember. That was one success story.

Translated, it meant the House of Treasure. And it truly was. She made sure to have all the popular current books as well as many classics. Anyone could find a treasure there. Regardless of what they sought.

Her love life, however, was not a success story. And with three months until she turned forty, she was beginning to wonder if all those long hours at the store neglecting desires and commitments had been worth it. On the best of days, she knew it had. Today was a hard day, though. She couldn't put her finger on it, but the day just didn't feel good. And neither did she.

As she gazed into the flames, she thought of the hidden room she'd discovered below the bookshelves those many years ago. She wondered anew about the golden box that she'd never been able to open. It was locked and appeared that it would only open if she could find a cursive R to match the one on the lock. God knows, she'd tried. Sure, she could have gotten a locksmith to try to get it open, but somehow that seemed disrespectful to whoever had placed it there.

There was no point thinking about that now. She didn't have a cursive R, and she hadn't been in the room in months. Maybe she'd go in later today. Would that improve her mood? Who knew? At least it was something different than the mundane existence she lived.

The bells on the front door tinkled and she knew she didn't need customers seeing her simply sitting in front of the fireplace drinking coffee. She went behind the counter and opened the door to her office.

Rain pummeled the windows, and the trees she could just make out were bent almost in two from the force of the wind. She had to turn on the light. It was extremely dark in the office, which didn't help her mood.

The books balanced. No surprise there. Gabby was wonderful as the manager of the store. She kept the other employees, all three of them, in line. While Lisette did all the hiring, she left the training in Gabby's capable hands. Gabby had been at the store for five years now. It didn't seem possible. Time flew. Gabby had come as a university student looking for a part-time job. They'd hit it off at once and Gabby had been there ever since.

The bookstore did a thriving business which meant Lisette was able and more than willing to pay Gabby a living wage. The other employees were part-time. Two young women and a young man, Louis, helped run the place. They worked hard and most had become quite good at memorizing authors' names and their works.

Louis, a history major, loved that Lisette had many classics there from authors in every corner of the world. Louis's personal favorite to read and recommend was *Le Père Goriot* by Balzac. He considered it a great novel that was also a great way to discover French culture. Lisette agreed and loved watching Louis's face light up when anybody asked for a recommendation from him.

After Lisette had compiled a list of books she wanted to take to the bookfair, she took the list out into the brightly lit area behind the counter and handed it to Gabby.

"Check this out, okay? Let me know if you see any we shouldn't take or if you can add any we need to."

"Not a problem."

"I heard customers come in a while ago," said Lisette. "Did they buy anything?"

"A map of Quebec City. At least that's something."

"Oui. It is indeed."

"I'm going to explore the hidden room," Lisette said. "I'll be back. If you need me, text."

"Will do. May I ask why you're going there? Did you get an idea for opening the box?"

"I wish." Lisette laughed. "I don't know. I just feel like looking around."

"Whatever. You're the boss."

"I am indeed." Lisette laughed again and went back into her office.

Her office was decorated in dark woods and green leather. It was comfortable and professional at the same time. Pictures on the walls were of different sights around the famous walled city she called home.

One wall, however, held no pictures. There was no space for them. The wall was covered by a floor to ceiling bookshelf. She pulled out the French book of fairy tales and the left side of the bookshelf moved forward, revealing a steep set of stairs.

Lisette grabbed the flashlight from her desk and descended the stairs. She arrived in a dusty room that was just larger than her office. It smelled dank and mildewy. She wished there were windows to air it out, but there were not. There was nothing that would make it visible to the outside world.

She shined her light around the space, focusing on the pictures on the wall. They were all of the French revolution. Lisette made a mental note to let Gabby know in case she needed fodder for the fliers she was creating.

One picture drew Lisette to it, as usual. It was a painting of Marie Antoinette at the guillotine. She wondered anew who built this room and why the fascination with the revolution? And why on earth would anyone want a painting of a guillotine about to fall? It was macabre. Yet it fascinated her.

The other paintings were of the crowds storming the Bastille and Liberty leading the revolution. There were other, smaller paintings, but those were the main ones. Lisette studied each one carefully hoping to find a clue as to why the room existed.

She crossed the room to the large, solid wood desk very similar to Louis XVI's. It had more drawers than his but was quite sturdy. Lisette dusted off the leather high-back chair and sat. She dragged her fingers tenderly over the Holy Bible and another book, too faded to know what it originally was.

Lisette carefully untied the pack of letters and read them for the umpteenth time.

*My darling Margot,*

*I hope you made it to what's been called New France. I do hope you've kept your promise, and everything is safe. I miss you and hope you're well. Please reply this time.*

*Love,*

*Josephine*

Who were these women? How old were these letters? The reference to New France made it obvious they were very old. She knew Canada was called that until 1763. She imagined these letters were written around that time.

She read more letters, all from Josephine. Some of them were clearly replies, others seemed to be pleading for a response. Who was Margot? Why hadn't she responded? Once again, Lisette promised herself to do some research on them. And what was it Margot was supposed to keep safe? Would Lisette ever get to the bottom of it?

Finally, she pulled the mysterious gold box close. It was well put together as Lisette could see no hinges. It was a solid box. In the front was what appeared to be a button with a cursive R on it. Was there a signet ring somewhere that opened it? She had tried making a wax stamp of the letter and pressing it to the R, but that had only made a mess. There had to be a way to get it open. She simply hadn't thought of it yet.

Her phone buzzed, startling her. When her heart had slowed down to a normal beat, she checked it. Gabby needed her. She went back up the stairs, replaced the book on nursery rhymes, and left her office to see what Gabby needed.

Sheridan Rousseau hurried down the Rue Saint-Jean, wanting to get out of the rain.

"Wait, Dr. Rousseau," Sarah, called. "I can't keep up."

Sheridan stopped and waited for her assistant to catch up to her. Sarah was five foot four inches, where Sheridan was an even six feet. Her strides were long and confident, and she felt sorry for Sarah. However, she was getting drenched in the deluge and wanted to find a place to escape the weather.

"There's a bookstore." Sarah pointed to a shop a few doors down. "Maybe they have coffee. We can warm up and relax for a few minutes."

Sheridan's stomach growled. She needed food, but respite from the storm would also be nice.

"Great. Come on."

Sheridan opened the door and let Sarah enter first. When Sheridan closed the door behind them, she inhaled deeply and was greeted by the scents of fresh coffee and books. Two of her favorite things.

She followed the smell of the coffee to the counter along the back wall. There were two pots of coffee there, as well as some pastries. Bingo.

"You are a genius," she said. "This was a most excellent suggestion."

Sarah blushed a little and smiled.

"I try," she said.

They helped themselves to coffee and Sheridan took two pastries and they headed to the left where there was an expanse of books. Slowly, Sheridan took in all the categories of books: mystery, fiction, nonfiction, historical romance, medical.

"I'm going to look at the medical books," she said.

"Of course, you are." Sarah laughed. "I'll be in the historical romance section."

Sheridan found an older version of an anatomy book and was sitting in an overstuffed chair reading it.

"Ah, the intellectual type, eh?"

She glanced up to see a petite brunette with pools of chocolate for eyes standing there. The woman was a beauty, which offset her annoyance at being interrupted.

"I'm Lisette. I own this bookstore," the woman said.

Sheridan stood and towered over the gorgeous woman.

"I'm Sheridan." She offered her hand.

"Ah. An American?"

"Yes. Your accent is unique though. Somewhat French, but I can't put my finger on it."

"I'm a native here. So, you hear a Quebec accent."

"It's very nice."

"Thank you. Now, please sit down. Be comfortable. I didn't mean to take so much of your time," said Lisette.

"No apology necessary. It's a pleasure to meet you. Please, pull up a chair and join me."

Lisette eyed a large, overstuffed chair a few shelves over.

"Wait here," said Sheridan. "I'll get it."

Years of working out came in handy as Sheridan picked up the chair and brought it next to hers. She was careful not to put them too close together. Although she was sorely tempted to. She wanted to touch this Lisette woman. She craved physical contact from her. It was at precisely that moment she realized that her dedication to her profession as a neurosurgeon had denied her pleasures she deserved.

"I'm impressed. Smart and strong? Two very attractive qualities." Lisette blushed. Sheridan wondered if she was flirting with her. If so, was Sheridan brave enough to flirt back? Did she even remember how?

Once seated, Sheridan decided to start slowly. She was infinitely curious about Lisette, and even wanted to ask her out, but what did she know of her? Nothing. Just that she was stunningly beautiful with a voice that could melt a glacier.

"How long have you owned this place?" Sheridan said.

"Seven years now. I saved and saved and still couldn't afford it until I was thirty-three."

So she was forty. Only three years Sheridan's junior. Perfect. Perfect for what? Sheridan asked herself. Why was she so smitten?

"What brings you to Quebec City?" Lisette said.

"I am here for a conference at the university. It starts tomorrow. Sarah and I decided to get acquainted with the city today before the heavens opened up." She didn't miss the slight frown on Lisette's face and hurried to add, "Sarah is my assistant."

Relief shown on Lisette's features. They continued talking with Lisette inquiring about what Sheridan did for a living and sharing stories of growing up in the walled city where neighbors still looked out for each other.

"It's an American saying, no? It takes a village to raise a child? Well, that's how it was growing up here. The whole neighborhood looked out for each other."

"I'd love that. You're lucky."

"Oh, Sheridan, was your childhood not magical?"

Sheridan didn't feel like discussing her childhood, having been raised by a single, alcoholic father.

"America is not as quaint at Quebec City, I'm afraid."

"So I've heard."

Sarah walked up then.

"Dr. Rousseau? Are you ready for lunch? I know you were hungry earlier."

"Oh, if you two are going to lunch, I have the perfect recommendation for you," said Lisette.

"Oh, Lisette, this is my assistant, Sarah. Sarah, this is Lisette. She owns the bookstore."

"How cool! This place is amazing," said Sarah.

Sheridan wanted Sarah to disappear again, but she had to admit the pastries hadn't done much to fill her up and lunch appealed.

"You were recommending a place for us to eat?" Sheridan said.

"Oui. You need to check out Cochon Dingue. It has delicious, authentic French food."

"That sounds fantastic." Sheridan wasn't actually being truthful. Outside of crepes, she had no idea what French food even was. "Would you like to join us?"

"I wouldn't want to intrude."

"No intrusion at all," Sheridan said.

"Actually," Sarah said. "I'm really into this book I found. You two go on ahead. I'll be there a little later. I'm not all that hungry, but I know Sheridan is famished."

"Are you sure?" said Lisette. "I don't mean for you not to come."

"I'm sure. You two go. Have fun. Educate Sheridan on another culture."

Sheridan laughed.

"Thanks, Sarah. Come on, Lisette. Lead the way."

## CHAPTER TWO

The rain had slowed to a drizzle, but still Sheridan gladly held an umbrella for the two of them as they walked down the street to the restaurant. The menu was in French, so Sheridan had to ask Lisette to translate. Lisette didn't seem to mind as she read each item and described them in English.

"It all sounds so good. What do you recommend?" said Sheridan.

"This or this." Lisette pointed to two items.

Sheridan thought about it and finally told Lisette what she wanted and asked her to order for her. Lisette politely agreed with a smile that warmed Sheridan to her core.

They chatted amicably and sipped white wine until the food arrived, then Sheridan dug in. She was starving and absolutely loving her meal. She managed to come up for air after a few minutes.

"This is delicious," she said. "How is yours?"

"Absolutely wonderful."

"I'm sorry I've been so focused on devouring lunch rather than you. I don't mean to be rude."

"You're not." Lisette laughed. "I love a woman who enjoys good food."

"And this is the best."

"It's not as good as home cooked," said Lisette. "But I agree, it's very good."

"Don't tell me you cook on top of owning your own bookstore? When do you have the time?"

"I make the time. Not often, I must confess. But Gabby is a highly capable manager, so if I want to cook a decent dinner, she lets me leave early so I can do that."

"I'd love to taste a home cooked French meal," said Sheridan.

"Then come for dinner tonight."

"Are you serious?" Sheridan couldn't believe her ears. Was Lisette inviting her to her house? What could that mean? She could only hope it meant more than the words said.

"Sure. I mean, if you don't find me too forward. I'd love to cook for you."

"That sounds amazing. Where? What time?"

"Well, this lunch will stay with us for a while. So, let's say seven?"

"Perfect."

"And may I have your phone?" Lisette said.

Sheridan handed over her phone.

"I've entered my phone number and address. I can have Gabby pick you up, though, if you'd like."

Sheridan's heart sunk.

"Will Gabby be joining us?"

"Oh, no." Lisette laughed. "But I know she'd happily give you a ride if need be. There are plenty of taxis in the city, but the drivers don't all speak English very well."

"I appreciate it, but I'll take my chance with the taxi."

Lisette beamed at her and Sheridan's breath caught. She was gorgeous. Fucking gorgeous. And she had invited her to her house for dinner. Sheridan began making plans to skip the conference the next day.

"I should get back to the store, unfortunately," said Lisette. "I need to make sure Gabby is okay and that Louis showed up for his shift. Then, I'll leave to go shopping and get started on dinner."

"Can I give you some money for the ingredients?"

"Nonsense. I'm happy to buy them and prepare a meal. It won't be a heavy meal. I promise. But I hope you'll enjoy it."

"I'm sure I will. I'll bring the wine. Red or white?"

"White, please."

"Will you tell me what we're having?" said Sheridan.

"No, I will not. It shall be a delicious surprise."

"Fair enough." Sheridan laughed. She couldn't remember the last time she'd enjoyed herself this much. She was thoroughly enthralled by Lisette. And she wanted to spend every moment possible with her.

They walked back to the bookstore. The rain had stopped, and the sun was trying to fight through the clouds.

"We may get a decent evening, after all," Lisette said.

"It will be more than a decent evening. Of this, I'm sure."

"No pressure, eh?"

"None. Okay, I need to find Sarah and let her know my plans. I'll see you at seven?"

"Sounds good. See you then."

Lisette walked over to the counter where several customers were checking out. Louis was charming them while he rung up their sales. Gabby was nowhere to be seen. Lisette needed to find her. She sent her a text. Gabby answered immediately that she was in the children's section.

Lisette walked into the small alcove that held children's books, as well as stuffed animals, and a track with cars for the children to play on. There were several small picnic tables in the alcove, as well. Perfect for kiddos to sit and read.

Gabby was there, taking books off the tables and replacing them where they belonged.

"Gabby, were we busy while I was out?"

"Somewhat. Nothing we couldn't handle. It was the two families with like six or seven kids that came through here like a tornado."

"I see. Let me help you."

Gabby looked at Lisette then.

"I've got this." She grinned. "You look happy. How was your date?"

Lisette felt the heat rise to her cheeks.

"It was wonderful. And I'm making dinner for her tonight. So, I'll be leaving now. I have my phone with me if you need me."

"I won't. But I'm worried. What do you know about this American? Is it safe to invite her to your place? What if she's a crazy person?"

Lisette laughed.

"She's not. Trust me."

"You look happy. Really happy. I'm. happy for you. But I worry."

"I promise I'll text you if things go sideways."

"I hope you'll call the police first, *then* text me."

Lisette laughed again.

"I appreciate your concern, but I assure you, I won't need the police."

"I feel like I should vet her first," said Gabby.

"No need. She's a doctor. She's sweet. She's amazing."

"She *says* she's a doctor. But how do we know?"

"I've already googled her." She showed her phone to Gabby. "See? Her picture doesn't do her justice, but it's clearly her."

"Fair enough," said Gabby. "Just be careful."

"Careful is my middle name."

"Well, at least that much is true."

"Okay. I'm heading out. I'll see you in the morning."

"Text me if you're going to be late or I'll worry."

"Yes, ma'am."

Lisette hummed to herself as she walked through the farmer's market and the fish market and picked up what she'd need for dinner. She walked back to the bookstore and got her car from the parking lot in the back. After stashing her goodies in the back seat, she drove home.

She spent the afternoon chopping herbs and preparing the souffle. Next, she mixed the smoked salmon with cream cheese, Dijon mustard, horseradish, and lemon and placed it in the refrigerator to cool.

Everything was ready to put in the oven or serve by five thirty, so she quickly picked up and vacuumed. Then, she took a hot shower and dressed in a long sage skirt and a white peasant blouse. She examined herself in the mirror and was happy with the woman who smiled back at her. She slipped on her favorite pair of Birkenstocks and called herself ready.

It was six forty-five and her nerves finally kicked into high gear. What the hell was she doing, anyway? For one thing, Gabby was absolutely right. She didn't know Sheridan from Adam's house cat. And, more importantly, perhaps, she didn't know if Sheridan played on her team.

Though Sheridan was tall, thin, with somewhat broad shoulders. She wore her dark hair short. She *looked* like a lesbian. And she certainly had Lisette's gaydar pinging. If she wasn't queer, well, Lisette would be disappointed, but at least she'd have made a new friend.

Not that a new friend would ease the aching between her legs that had roared to life when Sheridan had stood to introduce herself. But it had been so long, Lisette wasn't sure she'd remember what to do in bed with a handsome woman. She needed to cool her train of thought. Nobody said anything about sex. Sheridan was coming for dinner. That was it.

The doorbell rang at precisely seven o'clock. Lisette smoothed imaginary wrinkles out of her skirt and answered the door. There stood a vision she would never forget.

Sheridan was wearing black trousers, a gray blazer with a lavender shirt, and a skinny black tie. She looked delectable. She handed Lisette some flowers and Lisette snapped out of her mesmerized state and invited Sheridan in.

"The house smells fantastic. Have you been cooking all afternoon?" said Sheridan.

"Not all afternoon. Not really. I just hope it tastes as good as it smells."

"I'm sure it will. By the way, you look marvelous."

"Thank you. You cleaned up quite nicely yourself. That shirt really brings out your eyes. What color is that exactly?" Lisette said.

"The shirt? Or my eyes?" Sheridan teased her.

"Your eyes, goofball. They're almost purple."

"They are violet," Sheridan said. "But they tend to shift shades depending on what I'm wearing."

"Yes. I see that. Well, they're beautiful, whatever they are." Lisette blushed after realizing what she'd blurted out.

"Thanks. They work. That's all I can ask for."

"Come on into the kitchen and please pour the wine. I'll take the souffle out. You're welcome to help yourself to the salmon rillettes."

"The what?"

Lisette laughed.

"The salmon spread on the crostini."

"Is that what this is?" Sheridan pointed to the pink dip looking thing.

"Indeed. Here. Allow me to demonstrate." Lisette spread some of the salmon mixture onto the crispy crostini. She placed the tip of it in Sheridan's mouth. "Try this."

Sheridan took a bite and immediately let out an appreciative "Mm."

"Ah, so you like?"

"Yes, ma'am. Very much."

"Good. This is only the appetizer. Please enjoy."

Lisette took the souffle out of the oven and carried it to the table with oven mitts so Sheridan could see it in all its beauty. She was quite proud of how it turned out and was careful not to let it sink.

"That looks amazing," said Sheridan.

"Thank you. It won't last, so please serve up. I'll be right back."

Lisette took a moment to compose herself in the kitchen. Her heart was hammering, and she could barely breathe. These sensations hadn't happened to her in years. On one hand, she wanted to enjoy them. On the other, she had no clue if Sheridan was even remotely interested. She wanted to believe she was. Why else would she have come to dinner? Maybe she was just a friendly tourist?

When she got back to the table, she saw that the souffle had fallen slightly and that Sheridan hadn't served it yet.

"You didn't serve up?" she said.

"I don't know how to serve souffle. I'm sorry. I've heard of it but have never had it."

"No apologies necessary. Allow me."

Lisette stood next to Sheridan's chair. Dangerously close to Sheridan. So close she could feel the heat radiating off her. She took the long spoon and scooped out a helping for Sheridan. She placed it on her plate.

"Enjoy." Her voice was shaky, and she hoped Sheridan hadn't noticed.

Lisette had also set asparagus on the table, but neither of them touched it. They enjoyed several helpings of the souffle and had started on their second bottle of wine when Sheridan leaned back in her chair.

"No more. Oh, my God, was that delicious. But I'm afraid I can't eat another bite."

"It's okay. I'm in the same boat. Would you like a cognac by the fire?"

"That would be wonderful." Sheridan began clearing the table.

"Oh, please. Leave those. I'll get them."

"Nonsense. It's the least I can do. You get the cognac, okay?"

She carried everything to the kitchen while Lisette poured two cognacs from her crystal decanter.

"That's enough," she called from the living room. "Come join me, please."

They sat on the couch in silence and sipped the amber liquid.

"That was an amazing dinner," said Sheridan. "And now this? This is heaven."

"Why do I hear a 'but'?"

"I'm afraid it's getting late. And I do have a conference to attend tomorrow. I'd forgotten I'm speaking, or it wouldn't really matter. I can't speak to a group while I'm exhausted or hungover."

Lisette laughed.

"No. That wouldn't do at all."

"So, I'll say good night and thank you for a very lovely evening."

"I'll walk you to the door."

"May I come to the bookstore to see you tomorrow?"

"I'd like that," said Lisette.

"As would I."

They stood at the door in silence until a honk broke through the moment.

"Ah, my taxi is here," said Sheridan. "I'll see you tomorrow."

She leaned in slowly, deliberately. Lisette's heart raced and her breath caught. Sheridan kissed her cheek. The heat coursed through Lisette. She looked into Sheridan's eyes, begging for more.

"Good night, Lisette."

"Good night."

She watched Sheridan until the taxi drove off. She closed the door and squeezed her legs together to ease the throbbing. She had it bad.

## CHAPTER THREE

Sheridan woke to the shrill sound of her phone ringing. She checked the time. Seven thirty. She must have turned off her alarm. She saw it was Sarah calling.

"Hey, Sarah," she said.

"Thank God you're awake. I thought we were meeting for breakfast at seven fifteen. I knocked on your door and you didn't answer. Are you okay?"

"I am. I just overslept."

"The conference starts at eight."

"I'm aware," said Sheridan. "You go on. I need to take a shower and get ready. I'll be there by nine. I don't speak until ten anyway."

"Okay. I have your presentation with me. Text me when you get there."

"Will do. Thanks, Sarah."

Sheridan let out a heavy sigh. She needed to get a move on, and she so wasn't feeling it. As she stood in the shower, she allowed her mind to drift back to the events of the previous evening. It had been perfect. The only thing that would have made it better would have been if she'd woken up in Lisette's bed. There was something about Lisette that spoke to Sheridan on a very basic level. Sheridan was deeply attracted to her. It had been years since Sheridan felt the urges she was feeling now.

As she dried off, she asked herself what she knew about Lisette. Nothing, really. She owned a bookstore and made a mean souffle.

She could be a closet serial killer for all Sheridan knew. She smiled to herself. No. Lisette was sweet and kind and honorable. When Sheridan recalled the look in her eyes after she'd kissed her cheek, the ache in her belly was real. She knew Lisette had wanted more. She just hoped she'd have the opportunity to do more while she was there.

It was eight fifty-five when the taxi dropped Sheridan at the university. She found the lecture hall and was finally able to spot Sarah in the crowd. She made her way to her. Sarah handed her the slides that would accompany Sheridan's presentation.

Sheridan took them and excused herself to find an empty classroom where she could review her notes on her MacBook. After a half hour of review, she felt ready to take on the attendees. She would enlighten them on the most recent breakthroughs in neurosurgery. She was excited and couldn't wait to begin.

The crowd got to their feet when Sheridan concluded her presentation. She thanked them all and assured them she'd be at the presenters' table Friday evening if anyone had questions. She also wrote her email address on the board, just in case.

"You were amazing," Sarah said. "Like, oh my God, you blew them away."

"That was the plan. I couldn't have done it without your help."

"You're too kind."

"With your skills and my brains, we're unstoppable."

"Yes, we are," said Sarah. "Now, did you want to hear any other speakers?"

"Not particularly."

"What about food? You missed breakfast. You must be starving."

"That I am. Let's get some lunch. But, first, we need to drop all this off at the hotel."

"We can get lunch in the dining room."

"Actually," said Sheridan. "I'd very much like to go visit Lisette."

"The woman from the bookstore?"

"The very one."

"Dr. Rousseau, please be careful. You can't fall for someone who lives in another country."

"While I appreciate your concern, Sarah," said Sheridan, "it may be entirely too late."

"Wow."

"Don't sound so disappointed. There are worse women to fall for than a bookstore owner in Quebec City. And who knows? We're only here for a few weeks anyway."

"Forgive me, ma'am, but you don't strike me as the type who has a fling."

"I'm not. Let's just go see her. She may have already forgotten about me."

"As if," said Sarah.

"You know." Sheridan was getting tired of Sarah's doomsaying. "You don't have to go to the bookstore with me. You could have listened to more speakers. Or you could explore the city on your own."

"Are you kidding? I love that bookstore. Plus, I need to finish the book I started yesterday. Though, I think I'll buy it and go find a park to sit in. It's a beautiful day today."

"Let me buy you the book," Sheridan said. "It's the least I can do."

"That would be great. Thank you."

They exited the taxi and Sheridan stretched. The warmth of the sun felt amazing after the rain from the previous day. The temperature was in the high sixties but felt warmer in the direct sun.

"What a beautiful day," said Sheridan.

"Indeed. Now, let's get inside so you can buy that book for me."

Inside, Sheridan went straight to the back counter to see if Lisette was around.

"She's in her office," the young man behind the counter said. "I'll let her know you're here. What was your name?"

"I don't want to interrupt her. I'll see her when she comes out."

Sarah walked up then and handed Sheridan two books.

"I'm almost finished with *Singing with Magpies* so I need to get another to keep me occupied." Sarah laughed.

"Sounds good. Tell me." Sheridan read the man's nametag. "Louis. Is there a park nearby where Sarah can sit and read?"

"Oui. I'll show you after I ring these up."

Sheridan paid and Louis escorted Sarah outside and Sheridan watched him point and gesture. Sarah was smart and she was sure she'd find it. Sheridan made her way back to the medical books and found a section of journals. She found the recent ones and took one about neurology to a cozy chair and began reading.

"I heard a tall, mysterious American was looking for me," Lisette said.

Sheridan looked up and smiled, her face getting hot.

"You did, did you?"

"Oui. How are you today? I thought you had a seminar or something?"

"Yes. My presentation was well accepted, so we decided to come here to celebrate. I bought Sarah a couple of books and she headed to a park to read. I don't suppose I could talk you into a celebratory lunch?"

"That's great. And twist my arm. I'd love to join you for lunch."

"Excellent. Let me buy this." She held up the journal. "And we can head out."

"Neurology?"

"Yes. I'm a neurosurgeon."

"Oh, wow. You are way out of my league." She realized what she'd said and felt the heat rush to her cheeks.

"Nonsense," said Sheridan. "Now, let's get lunch."

"What are you in the mood for?"

"Something light. I'd like to take you out for a nice dinner tonight, if I may?"

"I'd like that. Something light. Let's go to a crepe house."

"Okay. That's a French word I understand." Sheridan laughed.

They walked the short distance to the crepe house.

"I love how close everything is here," said Sheridan.

"We are on the Rue Saint-Jean. Everything is within walking distance."

"I love this city. I have to tell you. It's magical."

"I'm thrilled you love it. It's my home and I love sharing it with you."

They ordered their lunch and sipped sparkling water.

"I'm bummed I couldn't talk you into a glass of wine," Sheridan said.

"I still have a long workday ahead of me."

"All work and no play..."

Lisette laughed.

"Tonight, we'll play."

"Promise?"

Lisette fumbled for an appropriate response. She couldn't think. The way Sheridan was looking at her with her intense violet eyes and one eyebrow arched, made it impossible to know what exactly she meant.

"I promise." It was a simple, noncommittal answer. Lisette wished she'd had the strength to say, "Define play." But she hadn't.

"Sounds good," said Sheridan. "I look forward to it."

*Damn her. She gives nothing away.*

Lunch was served and they ate in comfortable silence. When they'd finished, Lisette said, "I trust you enjoyed that?"

"Mm. Very much."

"Do you have any room left? We could split a dessert crepe."

"I think I have enough room for that."

They split a chocolate and strawberry dessert crepe which Lisette let Sheridan have the majority of. She loved to watch the look on Sheridan's face as she enjoyed every bite.

"You hardly touched it," said Sheridan. "Did you not enjoy it?"

"I did. But I can have these any time. They are a rarity for you."

"Well, thank you. It far exceeded my expectations."

"This makes me happy. Now, I need to get back to work. I'm sorry."

"It's okay. I understand."

As they walked back to the bookstore, Sheridan said, "So, where can I take you to dinner tonight? I want it to be fancy. I have a tux if I need to wear one."

"Sheridan, that's really not necessary."

"But it's something I want to do."

"Well, I appreciate it. I don't think a tux will be necessary, but if you want to go fancy, do you have a suit?"

"I do."

"Perfect. I'll make reservations for seven."

"Thank you," Sheridan said.

"My pleasure."

Sheridan took her hand and stopped her on the busy sidewalk. People gave them dirty looks as they made their way past.

"What's up?" Lisette tried to calm her fears, but they were racing to the forefront of her emotions.

"You have the most beautiful smile. I just needed to tell you that."

"Thank you." Lisette blushed. "I'm glad you like it."

"I really do."

"We should move. We're blocking people."

"Yes," said Sheridan. "We should."

She didn't let go of Lisette's hand, which thrilled Lisette in ways she couldn't put into words. Sheridan dropped her hand to open the bookstore door for her. Lisette immediately missed her touch.

"Thank you," Lisette said.

"My pleasure." Sheridan winked at her and her heart skipped a beat. If nothing else, Lisette hoped against all hope that Sheridan would kiss her that night. She needed to feel those lips on her.

"What are you going to do with the rest of your day?" Lisette said.

"I have a Q&A session I should get to. What time should I pick you up tonight?"

"Six forty-five?"

"Sounds good. I'll see you then."

Sheridan grinned at her before stepping out into a light drizzle.

"Who is she?" said Louis. "And, oh my God, could she be any more into you?"

"I don't know about that."

"Look at you. You're positively smitten."

"Louis!"

"You look like a schoolgirl with her first crush. I love it. You look like how I felt when I first met Jean Claude."

"I'm not smitten." Lisette tried to sound indignant.

"Liar."

"I'll be in my office if anybody needs me."

"I got you. You need some alone time after being with that tall, handsome drink of water."

Lisette slammed the door to her office but still heard Louis laughing. She collapsed into the wingback chair reserved for visitors. Louis was right. She was smitten. Or whatever the next step was. She was falling hard. For an American. She was an idiot. This couldn't work out.

Still, she should enjoy the time she had with Sheridan. She hoped Sheridan would spend the night. But then her conscience raised its ugly head. She wasn't the kind to sleep with a woman without a commitment. And she and Sheridan couldn't commit to each other. So, sex was off the table. Damn.

## Chapter Four

Sheridan was pleasantly surprised at the turnout for her Q&A. The attendees asked great questions, and she was happy to answer them. Sarah chose who would ask the questions and Sheridan answered them. They made a great team, and the hour session flew by.

"You were fantastic, Dr. Rousseau," said Sarah.

"That was fun. Speaking of fun, how was reading in the park?"

"It was great. Until it started raining. I swear it rains so much here."

"True statement."

"So, what's in store for the evening?" Sarah said.

"I'm taking Lisette out for a fancy dinner."

"Ma'am?"

"Yes?" Sheridan bit back.

"Ouch. No need to be defensive. I just worry."

"I'm an adult, Sarah. I can take care of myself."

"It's just that I've never seen you act this way. I don't want to see you get hurt."

"I won't. And neither will she. I promise you that," said Sheridan.

"I hope you're right."

"I am. Now, I need to get ready for my date. Will you be okay this evening?"

"Are you kidding me? I'm in love with this city. I may find a bar and go dancing."

"That sounds fun," said Sheridan. "Just be careful."

"You do the same."

"Will do. You want to share a cab back to the hotel?"

"Sure."

Back at the hotel, Sheridan soaked in the Jacuzzi tub before taking a hot shower. She imagined the thrill of showering with Lisette. She could almost feel Lisette's lithe body against her, those pert breasts there for her pleasure. Shit! She needed to get a grip. There was no guarantee she'd ever see Lisette naked. Which kind of sucked.

She dried off and dressed in a charcoal suit with a black shirt and gray tie. She blew her hair dry and applied a dab of gel to get a spikey look. She put on black socks and slipped into black loafers. She was ready.

She still had a few minutes. Cuff links? Why not. They had a signet R on them. They had been in her family for generations. She opened the drawer in her nightstand to get them and saw the matching signet ring. Why not? She felt even more ready. It was time.

Lisette opened her door looking positively stunning in a black, form-fitting cocktail dress. The heels she wore made her come up to Sheridan's eyes and Sheridan couldn't help but comment.

"How do you walk in those?" She laughed.

"Very carefully."

"I guess." Sheridan bent her elbow, and Lisette slipped her hand through.

They walked to the taxi and Sheridan opened the door for Lisette before she got in.

"Where to now?" said the driver.

Lisette said something in French and the driver smiled at them in the rearview mirror and gave a thumbs up.

"Is that the name of the restaurant?" Sheridan said.

"It is indeed."

"Great. I can't pronounce the name of the place. Am I going to be able to understand the menu?"

Lisette laughed and patted Sheridan's thigh. Sheridan felt the touch in the very core of her existence.

"They have English on the menu. You'll be fine."

"Oh, good. I've decided you're going to have to teach me French."

"Is that right?"

"I mean, if you don't mind."

"Not at all," said Lisette. "You don't have a lot of time left here. And I don't mind translating for you."

"Let's not talk about how much time I have left here. Let's just enjoy the time we have."

"Carpe diem," said the driver.

Sheridan wanted to be annoyed that the driver was listening to their conversation, but she had to agree with him.

"Yes," she said.

"Oui." Lisette smiled at Sheridan, and it took her breath away. She wanted to kiss her so desperately at that moment. But she didn't want an audience, so she fought the urge.

The taxi dropped them in front of a restaurant with a line out the door. It was cold and drizzly, and Sheridan did not want to stand outside and catch pneumonia. She knew, of course, that was an old wives' tale, but still.

"We have reservations," said Lisette. "Let's go in."

Inside, Lisette spoke in French to the maître d'. He smiled at her and waved a waiter over. The waiter took two menus, smiled at them, and said, "Right this way, s'il vous plaît."

"I understood that," Sheridan whispered in Lisette's ear.

"You've got this." She laughed.

"I don't have any idea what I want," said Sheridan.

"Let's start with escargot."

"Are you serious?"

"Of course. Have you never tried them?"

"No. And I don't see any reason to start."

"Trust me." Lisette smiled and Sheridan felt her heart melt.

"Okay. I will try one. But only one."

"If you say so."

"I tell you what. Why don't you just order for both of us? I do trust you and I can't seem to make a decision."

"You want French, right?" said Lisette.

"Yes. But preferably some red meat. Especially after the snails."

"You got it."

The sommelier arrived and looked to Sheridan to order the wine. She glanced at Lisette who merely smiled.

"We'll have two bottles of your finest red," said Sheridan.

"Oui. Good choice," he said.

The waiter stopped by and Lisette ordered a steak au poivre for Sheridan and a salmon meuniére for herself.

The sommelier was back with the wine for Sheridan to taste.

"That's very good," she said.

"Thank you. Your second bottle is decanting and will be ready when you are."

He poured them each a glass and was gone.

"I have to ask," Sheridan said. "What are we having for dinner exactly?"

"You're having a pepper encrusted steak and I'm having salmon in a brown butter sauce. We should both be extremely pleased."

"I'm sure we will be."

Lisette was finally relaxed enough to appreciate how handsome Sheridan looked. From her spiky hair to her tailored suit to her cuff links and ring. She was gorgeous and Lisette couldn't believe she was actually on a date with such a stunning woman.

Sheridan reached for her glass of wine and Lisette choked on her mouthful of wine.

"Are you okay?" said Sheridan. "You look like you've seen a ghost."

"I'm sorry. It's your ring."

"My signet ring?" Sheridan looked at the cursive R on her finger. "What about it?"

"Where did you get it?"

"It's been in my family for generations. I've heard rumors it dates back to the fifteen hundreds, but I have no proof. It's been passed to firstborn sons or only daughters over the centuries. I've managed to trace it back to about the French Revolution, but no further. I know at one point it belonged to a woman in the royal court."

"So you're the firstborn in your family?" Lisette tried to calm her racing heart.

"I'm the only child. What is your interest in my ring, though? Your eyes show more than mere interest. You look like you're about to devour my ring." Sheridan's laugh sounded nervous.

"I'm sorry. I know it's crazy. But, let me tell you a story."

"Sure."

"In my office, there is one wall that is covered by floor to ceiling bookshelves. When I first bought the place, I wanted to replace the books with some of my own. I was taking the books off the shelf one at a time. Some of them were quite old and I was fascinated by them.

"I removed an old book of French fairy tales and suddenly the bookshelf opened, revealing a dark staircase."

"Dang. Okay. You definitely have my attention now," Sheridan said.

"I followed the staircase and came to a room larger than my office. It was dark and dank and dusty. Oh, so dusty. It seemed no one had been down there in decades. Of course, I don't know how long it had actually been, but the secret room seemed abandoned."

"But you were safe, right? You didn't find a dead body or anything?"

Lisette laughed.

"No. Nothing like that. But there is a desk down there that has a gold box on it. The box is sealed. I've often thought of taking it to a locksmith, but I don't want to destroy it."

"Makes sense."

"So, here's the thing. There is an insignia indented in the front of this box. It's a cursive R. Just like, and I mean exactly like, the one on your ring. I saw it and couldn't help but wonder if it might open the box."

"You're serious?"

"I am," said Lisette.

"Then, after dinner, let's go there. We can try my ring. That is, if you don't mind?"

"If I don't mind? What about you? Are you sure you want to indulge my inner Hercule Poirot?"

Sheridan laughed.

"I'd love to. I hope it works. I wonder what's in the box. There's nothing down there indicating what it might be?"

"Not a thing. I should ask, just to be polite and because I'm curious. What does the R stand for?"

"Rousseau. It's my last name."

"So you do have some French in you. This makes me very happy."

"It does, does it?" Sheridan laughed.

"I like you, Sheridan. That shouldn't come as a shock. But I was having trouble reconciling my feelings with a name that might be English."

Sheridan laughed again.

"Sheridan is actually Gaelic. It means searcher."

"Searcher? Yes. That's wonderful. And a French last name makes everything better." She blushed.

"I take it you're an Anglophobe?"

Lisette shrugged.

"I'm French. What can I say?"

They laughed as their dinner was served. They ate in comfortable silence punctuated with delightful noises indicative of how much they were enjoying their meals. When they finished, they sat back, content.

"I take it your steak was good?" Lisette said.

"Oh, my God, yes. Not as good as the escargot, but delicious nonetheless."

"I knew you'd like those."

"I shall never doubt you again," said Sheridan.

Lisette laughed.

"Did you two save room for dessert?" The waiter was pushing a double-decker tray of deliciousness.

Sheridan arched an eyebrow at Lisette.

"Maybe we could split one?" Lisette said.

"Sure. Pick something decadent."

"Let's try the chocolate souffle."

"Excellent choice," said the waiter.

They took their time eating dessert, savoring every bite. When they had finally finished, Sheridan paid the bill, and they hailed a taxi to the bookstore.

The drive took them through the streets of the old walled city. Normally, Lisette would have chatted happily with Sheridan, pointing out all the sights, but all her energy was focused on the hidden room. She wondered if Sheridan's ring would actually open the box and, if it did, what they'd find inside. Money? Jewels? Her thoughts raced as she tried to know the unknown.

"You okay, babe?" Sheridan said.

"Hm?" She was roused from her revery and didn't miss Sheridan's term of endearment. It gave her warm fuzzies. "Yes. I'm just so excited to see if your ring opens the box. And I'm wondering what could possibly be in that box."

"I'm sure. I'm pretty excited, too. I feel like my ring could hold the answer to something big. And I've never even seen the box." She laughed.

"I know. We can't get our hopes up. I mean, realistically, what are the chances that your ring is going to open it?"

"This is true. But who's to say it won't?"

The taxi stopped in front of the bookstore.

"Well," said Lisette. "We're about to find out."

## CHAPTER FIVE

The bookstore was a little spooky in the dark, but it didn't seem to bother Lisette.

"Can we turn some lights on?" said Sheridan. "I can't see a thing."

"I suppose it's late enough that no one will think we're open. Let me turn on the overhead lights and lock the front door."

"Thank you. Now I feel like I'm where I'm supposed to be."

"Of course. Let's go to my office and down to the secret room."

Sheridan took Lisette's hand and felt her trembling.

"Calm down, babe. Either this works or it doesn't. But I don't want you having a stroke in the meantime."

Lisette laughed.

"I'm fine. Just excited."

Sheridan dropped her hand as she unlocked her office door and turned on the lights.

"You ready?" Lisette said.

"As I'll ever be."

She crossed the room to the bookshelf and pulled out a book. Sheridan watched as the bookshelf opened, revealing the hidden staircase. It wasn't that she'd doubted Lisette, but seeing it in person was a little overwhelming.

She began to wonder what she was doing there. How well did she know Lisette? How did she know Lisette wasn't guiding her to her doom? She shot Sarah a text letting her know where she was, just in case.

"Turn your phone flashlight on so you can maneuver down the stairs. There are lamps down below but no lights along the stairs," said Lisette.

"Gotcha."

At the bottom of the staircase, Sheridan stopped and looked around as Lisette turned on the lamps. The room was huge. There were more bookshelves lining the walls and paintings that looked centuries old. Her gaze came to rest on Lisette standing by a sturdy desk along the wall on the right. Sheridan crossed over to her.

"Here's the box," Lisette said.

Sheridan looked at it. It appeared to be solid gold. And sure enough, in the center of the front of it there was an indented cursive R.

"What do you think?" said Lisette. "Dare we even try?"

"What have we got to lose?" Sheridan slipped off her ring. She pressed it against the insignia on the box and heard a click. Her heart raced and she glanced at Lisette, whose hands covered her mouth. "Did you hear that?"

Lisette merely nodded.

"Well, come on then." Sheridan stepped back. "This is your baby. Go ahead and open it."

Lisette's hands shook visibly as she reached for the box. Sheridan heard Lisette's breath coming in shaky gasps. Sheridan stepped back, but only far enough for Lisette to get to the box. She stood behind her, pressed against her, curious to see what was inside.

Lisette opened the lid. There were three items inside. One was a piece of jewelry, one a vial of some sort, and the other appeared to be folded paper. Lisette touched the jewelry tenderly.

"It's yours now," said Sheridan. "Bring it out. Let's take a good look at it."

"It really is mine, isn't it?"

"It is."

"I feel like I'm intruding on someone else's possessions," said Lisette.

"No one else owns this bookstore. Whatever is in there is yours."

Lisette took the piece of jewelry out of the box and held it up so they could both see it.

"Is that a locket?" said Sheridan.

"Mm-hm." She opened it and her breath caught.

Sheridan could see a woman in it who appeared to be royalty based on the tiara and robe.

"Do you know who it is?" she said.

"I can't be sure," said Lisette. "But I'd bet my last dollar it's Marie Antoinette."

"Marie Antoinette? Wow."

"Let's take it upstairs where the light is better."

"Okay. But shouldn't we look at the paper, too? And what's in the vial?"

"Right." She reached back into the box and touched the remaining contents. "It doesn't feel like paper."

"What does it feel like?"

"Parchment of some sort."

"Unfold it," said Sheridan. "Let's see what it says."

Lisette did just that.

"I can't tell what it says," said Sheridan. "Can you?"

"I can't make it out. We'll take it upstairs, too."

"Sounds good. Come on. Wait. I have to ask. What's in the vial?"

Lisette opened the top and a lovely fragrance wafted out.

"It's Black Jade," she said. "It's what Marie Antoinette wore."

"Are you sure?"

"Positive."

"Wow. Okay, let's go upstairs and check out the parchment."

"Will you please turn off the lamps?" said Lisette.

"Of course. You head up. I'll be right there."

She turned off the three lamps and took the stairs two at a time. Lisette was clearing her desk.

"What are you doing?" she said.

"I want to lay this parchment flat so we can make sense of it."

"Did you look at the locket yet?"

"Yes. It's definitely Marie Antoinette."

"Wow. How long do you think that box has been sealed?"

"Obviously a very long time."

"I'd guess," said Sheridan.

Lisette spread the parchment on her desk. It was yellowed and discolored with age.

"I still can't tell what it is," she said. "I can kind of make out some lines or something."

"Here." Sheridan shined her phone flashlight on the parchment. It illuminated lines and some French words, but nothing that made any sense to Sheridan. "Does this help?"

Lisette shook her head.

"It still doesn't make any sense to me."

"Maybe we should sleep on it. Look at it again in the morning when we're rested."

"Maybe so," said Lisette. "Maybe it'll make sense in the light of day."

"Yeah."

"Okay. Let's get out of here."

"Do you have a safe or something?" said Sheridan.

"You think I should put them in there?"

"We don't know what it is. It may be worth something when we figure it out. Better safe than sorry."

"You're absolutely right."

Sheridan watched her put them away then cross back to her. Lisette stood mere inches from her. Sheridan's heart raced from the excitement and the closeness of Lisette.

"I don't know how to thank you."

"I didn't do anything." Sheridan shrugged. "I just happened to be wearing my ring. You're the one who noticed it and ran with it."

"But you believed me. You could have chalked me up as a crazy, delusional lady. But you didn't."

"Of course not. I believe in you."

"Sheridan?"

"Mm?"

"Will you kiss me?" said Lisette.

"I thought you'd never ask."

Lisette held her breath as she watched Sheridan's lips getting closer. What was she doing? She had no idea. All she knew was that she needed to taste those lips.

Their lips met and shock waves coursed through her body. It was everything she had fantasized about for the past couple of days. And more. Oh, so much more. She wrapped her arms around Sheridan's neck and pulled her closer. She never wanted the kiss to end.

Sheridan pulled away an inch and stared into Lisette's eyes. Lisette pulled her back to her and opened her mouth, begging Sheridan's tongue to enter. Sheridan complied and Lisette's world spun off its axis. This seemed so right. So natural. She might not know Sheridan well, but she knew she wanted her. With every ounce of her being. And she didn't want to wait.

"Come home with me," she whispered.

Sheridan rested her forehead on Lisette's.

"God, I want that."

"Then it's settled."

Sheridan chuckled.

"It's not that easy," she said.

"Why not?" Lisette stepped back.

"Lisette, I want you. I desperately want you. But we don't really know each other. And I'm not a one-night stand kind of girl."

"I don't want a one-night stand."

"What else can I give you? I'm only in town for a few weeks. Then what?"

Lisette looked at her feet.

"Damn. I hate reality sometimes."

Sheridan placed her finger under Lisette's chin and made her look at her.

"Reality is complicated. And nobody regrets that more than I do right now."

"Except maybe me."

"Yeah," said Sheridan. "I suppose you do, too."

"We should get a taxi to take us home. I promise not to kidnap you. I'll have them drop you at your hotel."

"I appreciate that."

"And," said Lisette, "just for the record, I'm not into one-night stands either."

"I didn't figure you would be."

"It's just that I haven't felt this way in so long. If ever."

Sheridan squeezed her eyes tight.

"You're not making this any easier," she said.

"Okay. Let's get out of here. Will you come by in the morning to look at the parchment with me?"

"I wouldn't miss it."

Sheridan brushed her lips over Lisette's again and Lisette felt her knees go weak. She rested her head on Sheridan's chest.

"We'd better get going," Sheridan said at last.

The taxi ride went far too quickly for Lisette's liking. Sheridan kissed her briefly before getting out at her hotel. Lisette rested her head against the backseat and closed her eyes. Damn. What was she going to do?

Alone in her house, Lisette was lonelier than she could ever remember being. She walked to her bedroom but couldn't make herself lie on the king-sized bed. Instead, she went into the bathroom and ran a hot bubble bath.

She soaked until she was a prune, then rinsed off in the shower. Tomorrow, she thought as she climbed into bed. She'd see Sheridan again tomorrow. And they'd look over the parchment together. The parchment. What did it mean? But thoughts of Sheridan's lips pushed all thoughts of the parchment out of her mind.

She slept fitfully and woke groggy. She made a pot of coffee, drank the whole thing, showered, then drove to the store. Sheridan and the parchment battled for position in her brain. She didn't know which she was more excited for.

"Morning, boss," said Gabby.

"How are you this morning?"

"Good. Hey, did you work late last night?"

"Why do you ask?"

"You forgot to turn the lights off in your office."

"Oh, yes. I came back here after dinner," said Lisette.

"Are you okay? You're not like, depressed or anything are you?"

"No. Why?"

"The last time you spent beaucoup hours here was after your dad died."

"Oh, no," said Lisette. She contemplated telling Gabby what she and Sheridan had found but opted not to. She wanted to keep it between Sheridan and herself for the time being. "Nothing like that. I just had something to check on."

"Good. I worry, you know. So, how was dinner?"

Lisette blushed thinking of her night before.

"It was wonderful."

"Damn, woman. You've got it bad."

"I'm afraid I have."

"And she's an American," said Gabby.

"That she is. Oh, well."

"Be careful, boss."

It was much too late for that, but she didn't speak that out loud.

"Thanks, Gabby. Okay. I need to get to work."

"Yes, ma'am. Oh. Before I forget, I drew up some flyers for the bookfair."

"Excellent. Let me see them."

Lisette was admiring all the samples Gabby had provided and didn't even hear the bell on the door chime.

"You two look busy. Should I come back later?"

Lisette almost got whiplash from looking up so quickly at the sound of Sheridan's voice.

"Look at these." She tried to sound cool. "These are some drawings Gabby did for the bookfair that's coming up."

"Wow," Sheridan said. "You're very talented."

"Thank you," said Gabby.

"I'm glad I don't have to be the one to choose. They're all amazing."

"We don't have to decide right now," said Lisette. "Come on into the office, Sheridan."

"Lead the way."

Alone in the office, Lisette stepped close to Sheridan.

"Kiss me?"

Sheridan kissed her hard and Lisette worried her lips would be bruised. Not that she cared. She wanted more and more from Sheridan and there had to be a way to get it.

"Let's check that parchment out again," Sheridan said when they finally came up for air.

Lisette got it out of the safe and spread it across her desk.

"It's no use," she said. "We're never going to figure out what it is."

"I have an idea. Will you turn on your desk lamp?"

Lisette reached under the shade and turned it on.

Sheridan placed the middle portion of the parchment on top of the lamp.

"Wow," she said. "Look at this."

Lisette leaned over and gasped.

"Oh, my God. I can't believe we found this."

## CHAPTER SIX

R ight? It's a map. But of what?" said Sheridan.
        "I can't really tell. It's in French, which isn't a problem, but it's old and faded and I can't make out much of it. This could take some time to figure it out."

"Hm. Well, can we get started figuring it out now?"

"I should do my morning work first. Why don't you settle out in the medicine section, and I'll come and find you when I'm ready."

"Sure. I smelled coffee out there, so I'll have some and find something to keep my mind occupied."

Lisette kissed her.

"Let that occupy your mind," she said.

"Oh, it will."

Sheridan spoke to Gabby at the counter.

"Hey there, could I get a cup of coffee, please?"

"As much time as you're spending here, you should have your own coffee cup."

Sheridan laughed. She didn't care that she and Lisette were obvious.

"Maybe I'll bring one by," she said.

"In all seriousness?" said Gabby.

"Sure."

"Don't hurt her."

"You have my word."

"In that case," Gabby said. "Here's your coffee."

"Thank you. Now, if a person was looking for an old map of Quebec City or even just Quebec, would there be a book here that could help?"

"How old are we talking?"

"Old, old."

"Well, the atlases are that way. I guess I'd start there." She pointed off to her left. Sheridan had never been over there before. She took her coffee and a pastry and headed off.

"Thanks," she called over her shoulder.

She perused the shelves until she found one that had "ancient" maps. She pulled it down and flipped through the pages. It was maps of Mesopotamia. And then Egypt and Greece. A little too ancient. She put it back.

She found another atlas, *Quebec Over the Years*. That looked promising. She was lost in the pages of maps when Lisette found her.

"So much for medicinal journals, huh?" Lisette smiled.

"I want to know what that's a map of. I have a feeling it has something to do with here. Why else would it have been left here, you know?"

"Makes sense."

"So, let's buy the book and talk about it over lunch. My treat."

"It seems all we do is eat."

"I can think of other things we could do." Lisette winked.

"Lunch it is."

Lisette laughed.

"Okay. Let's go."

"Let me buy this book first," Sheridan said.

"If you insist."

"I do."

They stepped onto Rue Ste-Jean. It had started to rain so Lisette opened her umbrella, and Sheridan held it over both of them. They hurried to a small bistro and ordered lunch. Sheridan opened the book and placed it on the table so Lisette could see it.

"I still don't know what we're looking at," Lisette said. "It's not like we're going to find that map in here."

"No. But we might find a map that is a similar shape. Or we might see some words we recognize. I don't know. It's just an idea."

"That makes sense now that you explained it. I'll flip through the maps and see what I can find."

Sheridan sat in silence, sipping her coffee, and watching Lisette carefully scour every map. Lisette was truly beautiful. And she was smart. And successful. She was everything Sheridan would look for in a woman if she had ever stopped and thought about letting someone in her life. Why hadn't she dated in the past ten years? Ten? At least. She'd dedicated herself to school and her career.

Here she was daydreaming about spending more time with, possibly sharing a life with a woman who lived in a different country. Fate was a bitch. Would Sheridan be strong enough to avoid taking Lisette to bed? Because that was the only thing she truly wanted. Besides maybe finding what the map was about.

"I don't know." Lisette closed the book as lunch was served. "So far I'm coming up empty."

"You're only halfway through the book."

"If that." Lisette laughed.

"There's still hope. Now eat up."

After lunch they strolled along the street and darted in and out of shops.

"I want to buy you something," Lisette said.

"Like what?" Sheridan laughed.

"I don't know. Something to remember me by."

Sheridan stopped in the middle of the sidewalk. People passing by bumped into them and there was more than a little swearing.

"I don't need anything to remember you by," said Sheridan. "I'll never forget you, Lisette."

Lisette pulled Sheridan into the street and kissed her.

"I'll remember you always as well," she said.

They arrived back at the bookstore cold and damp. The wind wasn't too strong, but it was blowing hard enough to get them wet even under the protection of the umbrella. Sarah and Gabby were chatting back at Gabby's station.

"What are you doing here?" Sheridan said.

"I texted you and asked if you were going to the convention today. You didn't answer so I figured I'd find you here. And here you are."

"Indeed. You're a wise woman, Sarah." She laughed.

"Right? You're rubbing off on me. So, what are we doing today?"

"We just had lunch. You should get something to eat."

"Let's grab lunch together," said Gabby.

"I'd like that."

"Great. Is that okay with you, boss?"

"That's great," said Lisette. "Take your time. Enjoy yourselves."

"Interesting," Sheridan said when they were out of earshot.

"Why? They can get lunch without it meaning anything."

"Did you see the smile on Sarah's face? She was positively glowing."

"Well, good for them. Quebec City seems to be a good place to fall for people."

"That it does," said Sheridan. "You know, those two are intelligent women. Maybe we could ask for their help."

"I don't know. That's kind of a big ask."

"I don't know Gabby like you do, but I believe Sarah would really sink her teeth into it."

"Oh, Gabby would be like a dog with a bone."

"Then let's invite them to help us."

Lisette contemplated what Sheridan was saying. On one hand, she really enjoyed it being something between the two of them. On the other hand, four heads were better than two.

"Okay. When they get back from lunch. I'll have Louis man the register and we'll show Gabby and Sarah the map."

"Excellent. Now, what should we do while we wait?"

"We could make out. Maybe I'd even let you cop a feel."

"Holy shit. You drive a hard bargain."

"Just a thought." Lisette grinned.

"And my brain just exploded."

"I knew we'd be explosive together." She laughed. Sheridan joined her. "I wonder where Louis is. I need him to watch the register now so we can be alone in the office."

"Settle your hormones."

"I don't want to."

Louis walked up with a customer and handed three books to Lisette. To the customer, he said, "You're going to love these books. And we have plenty more in this genre, so please come back and buy more."

"I will," said the customer.

"Actually, Louis," said Lisette. "Do you mind ringing these up? I have something I want to show Sheridan in the office."

"Not a problem. Where's Gab?"

"She's at lunch."

"Good for her. Sure. I'll watch the register."

Lisette and Sheridan walked into the office. Lisette locked the door. Sheridan arched an eyebrow at her. She took Sheridan's hand and led her to the couch. She sat down and crossed her legs, fully aware that her skirt had hiked up, showing off her thighs.

Sheridan sat next to her. Lisette watched Sheridan's gaze take in her thighs, breasts, and finally her eyes.

"Do you like what you see?" Lisette said.

"You know I do."

"Are you going to kiss me?"

"Is it safe?"

"Does it matter?"

"Damn. At this moment, I'm not sure," said Sheridan.

"Then kiss me and let fate take us where she may."

Sheridan leaned over and kissed Lisette. Softly at first, but soon, she was running her tongue over Lisette's lips and Lisette opened her mouth and welcomed her in. She took Sheridan's hand and placed it on her breast. She felt Sheridan moan into her mouth.

Sheridan closed her hand over Lisette's breast and squeezed gently. Lisette felt the squeeze all the way down to where her legs met. She needed Sheridan in a big way. She understood what was stopping them, but she also didn't care. At that moment, Sheridan could have done anything she wanted, and Lisette would simply have lay back and enjoyed.

She avoided interrupting Sheridan as she unbuttoned her blouse. She held it open, and Sheridan placed her hand inside. Lisette felt her nipple stiffen. It was almost painful. She quit kissing Sheridan and guided her mouth down to her breast. Sheridan peeled down Lisette's bra and sucked her nipple.

"Holy fuck," Lisette breathed. "Sweet, holy fuck you feel good."

Sheridan ran her hand down and cupped Lisette's ass. Lisette needed her hand on her, in her. She hiked her skirt up until it was around her waist. She placed Sheridan's hand on her hot, wet, throbbing center.

Sheridan sat up.

"No. Our first time will not be on the couch in your office."

"I can't think of a better place. Please, Sheridan. I need you."

"I won't, Lisette. I can't. I'm sorry." She got off the couch and left the office.

Lisette put herself together and fought tears. Her need was so intense. Never in a million years would she have believed herself capable of behaving so wantonly. But she was crazy about Sheridan and wanted to consummate whatever it was they had.

When her legs quit shaking, she walked out into the main area and found Sheridan chatting with Gabby and Sarah as if nothing had just happened. How could she be so cool?

"There she is." Sheridan kissed Lisette. "I was just telling them we had a top-secret mission we wanted to include them in."

"And I was just hoping it wasn't a foursome, because that could be awkward," said Gabby.

They all laughed, and Lisette relaxed a little. She was still throbbing, but she had to get her mind off that and onto safer territory.

"Yes," she said. "Well, not to the foursome. But we do have something we're working on, and we could really use your help."

"I'm all ears," said Sarah.

"Where did Louis disappear to?" Lisette said.

"He's helping some customers. Why?" Gabby said.

"I want him to watch the register while we go into the office where we can show you what we're working on."

"Can't you bring it out here?" said Gabby.

"I'd rather not."

"Show me how to work the register," Sheridan said. "I'll watch it while you three look at what's in the office."

"Thank you, but no," said Lisette. "We need to show them together."

Just then, up walked Louis.

"Talk about a meeting of the minds," he said.

"Hey, Louis, would you mind watching the register for a few?" Lisette said.

"Sure thing. Where are you four going?"

"We'll be in the office for a few. We won't be long."

## CHAPTER SEVEN

Inside the office, Lisette went to the safe and got the map out. She placed it on her desk.

"What is it? It looks old as hell," Gabby said.

"Hold it over the lamp," said Sheridan.

Gabby did and Sarah moved next to her.

"I'm still not sure what we're looking at," Sarah said.

"Neither are we," said Lisette. "But it appears to be a map or something."

"Are you sure?" said Gabby.

"Here." Sheridan moved between them and traced some of the lines that were visible.

"Ah," Sarah said. "I can see that now. But what is it a map of?"

"That's what we want your help to figure out," said Lisette.

"So, we need to figure out where the X is and what it means?" Gabby said.

"What X?" Sheridan moved over to join them. Sarah moved out of the way.

"Right there." Gabby pointed. "Doesn't that look like an X?"

"It really does. Lisette, come look at this." Lisette moved close to her and looked where she was pointing.

"Oh, my God. I think you're right. But where is that? And what is there?"

"The plot thickens," said Gabby.

"So, you want our help with this? What if we don't figure it out in the next few weeks? We have to leave soon." Sarah's words cut Lisette like a knife.

"I suppose we'll do everything we can to solve it while you're here," she said.

"I might stay on a little longer to help," said Sheridan.

"Do you mean that?" Lisette's heart skipped a beat.

"Sure."

"Well, if you're not at work, there's no reason for me to be there," Sarah said.

"Great. So, we'll work on this for at least a while then?" Lisette was more excited than ever.

"Okay," said Gabby. "So, we know there's an X, but we don't know what it's for or where it is. Is that about the sum of it? Where did you even find this map?"

"It was in the box in the secret room," Lisette said.

"Box? Secret room? What are you talking about?" said Sarah.

"Can I show her the secret room?" Gabby looked like a little kid at Christmas.

"Of course. Let me open the bookshelf for you."

"Open the bookshelf?" Sarah was clearly confused.

"Just wait," said Gabby.

Lisette took hold of the book of fairy tales and nursery rhymes and pulled it gently. The bookshelf opened and Sarah's eyes went wide.

"Go on," said Lisette.

Sarah looked at Sheridan.

"Have you been down there? Is it safe?"

"Completely."

Sarah turned and followed Gabby down the stairs.

"I knew getting them involved was a good idea." Sheridan put her arm around Lisette. Lisette leaned into her, wanting, craving more. But happy for what she could get.

"You were right. So now we know we're looking for something. At least there's some sort of light at the end of the tunnel."

"We'll figure it out."

The other two were back up the stairs.

"Was there anything else in the box?" said Gabby.

"As a matter of fact, there was." Lisette opened the safe and took out the locket and the perfume. She handed them to Gabby.

"Is that Marie Antoinette?" Gabby said.

"It is."

"What does that have to do with the map?" said Sarah.

"We have no idea. But if there is a connection, the four of us will find it," Sheridan said.

"Yeah, we will," said Gabby.

"This is a lot more fun than the convention." Sarah laughed.

"You're very right about that," said Sheridan. "I still have to speak tomorrow afternoon, but the rest of time, I say we focus on the map."

"We need to go to the library," said Gabby.

"I think you're right." Lisette put the locket and the map back into the safe.

"Why?" Sarah said. "I mean you guys have this bookstore. What could the library have that you don't?"

"More atlases and easier to find what we might need," said Sheridan. "I say we take the map to the library tomorrow morning."

"I don't like handling the map that much," Lisette said. "It's old and already falling apart. Plus, it's damned near impossible to read already. The more it's handled the worse it's going to get. Let's examine the map and then go get books. We can check out as many as we need."

"You're right. Of course." Sheridan kissed her. "You're so smart."

"You two certainly are chummy," Sarah said.

"We are. And now I think we should head back to the hotel. I need to get ready for dinner."

"You have dinner plans?" said Lisette.

"Well, I was hoping to have dinner with you."

"Hey," said Gabby. "Let's double date."

"Date?" Sarah said.

"Come on. You know you're into me." Gabby winked at her and Sarah blushed.

"Fine by me. That sounds fun," Lisette said.

"You two figure out where you want to go and let us know."

"Does this mean you'll give me your number?" Lisette laughed.

"Oh, yeah. I guess it does."

They exchanged phones and entered their numbers.

"See you all in a couple of hours," Sheridan said.

In the cab, Sarah looked at Sheridan very seriously.

"Do you know what you're doing?" she said.

"What exactly are you talking about? The treasure hunt?"

"No. I'm talking about you getting all lovey-dovey with a bookstore owner in flippin' Quebec City."

"What about you and Gabby?" Sheridan said.

"We're just having fun. I've never known you to have fun, so I'm assuming you're serious. And I'm wondering how wise that is."

"I can take care of myself."

"And Lisette? Can she take care of herself, too? Are you sure about that?" said Sarah.

"You let us worry about that, okay? Don't make me regret inviting you and Gabby on our treasure hunt."

They arrived at the hotel and Sarah got out of the cab and hurried inside. Sheridan paid the fare and walked slowly through the rain to the front door, giving Sarah plenty of time to get in the elevator so she didn't have to deal with her.

Sheridan respected Sarah very much and usually valued her input. Why was she so angry at her now? Maybe it was because Sarah's questions hit too close to home. Those were the same questions Sheridan had been asking herself. And she didn't have the answers. Would she ever? She was crazy about Lisette. She'd love to invite Lisette to move to the States to be with her, but how realistic was that? Sure, they were burning hot and heavy now, but would that translate to a relationship? If they didn't work, Lisette would be all alone in a strange country.

"Shit!"

Sheridan took a long, hot shower and tried to focus on the mysterious map. But her brain kept circling back to Lisette and their relationship, such as it was. Why did it take a trip to a convention in a foreign country to find the woman of her dreams? She hadn't felt this way in forever, if ever. She knew Lisette was the woman for her. So, what to do about that?

She dried off, dressed in charcoal slacks, a purple shirt, and a black blazer. Skinny tie in place, she checked her phone. There was a text from Lisette with the name of a restaurant and an address. Sheridan couldn't fight the smile. Lisette had texted her. Hopefully it would be the first of many.

She went down the hall and knocked on Sarah's door. No answer. Shit. Was Sarah going to continue with the attitude and ruin this night? Maybe a double date wasn't such a great idea after all.

Sheridan took the elevator to the lobby. There was a beautiful young lady standing with her back to her. She had a black dress on under a heavy coat. Sheridan couldn't help but admire the shape of the stranger's legs. Damn. She had to get some release soon. She was like a teenager with raging hormones, checking out strangers in the hotel lobby.

The woman turned around and smiled at her.

"Sarah? Damn, you clean up nicely."

"Thank you. So do you. Shall we?"

"Yes. Let's do this."

The ride to the restaurant was in mostly silence until Sarah finally spoke up.

"Were you serious about hanging in town a little longer if we need to to solve the mystery map?"

"I'm very serious."

"I'm really excited. I really want to know what the X stands for."

"You and me both, kid."

The taxi pulled up in front of an old stone building. They got out and hurried inside to get out of the downpour.

"Over here," Gabby said.

They crossed the lobby and said their hellos. Gabby hugged Sarah while Sheridan pulled Lisette into her arms. She kissed her forehead.

"You're beautiful," Sheridan said.

"And you're looking quite dapper tonight."

"Thank you."

"Your table is ready." The waiter stood with the menus, waiting for everyone to disentangle and follow him.

Their table was in the center of a large, glass-ceilinged room, right next to an expansive fountain with koi swimming at its base.

"This is impressive," said Sheridan.

"It's one of my favorite places," said Lisette. "I used to come here for coffee and to study while I was in school."

"I can see why," said Sarah. "It's peaceful."

"Exactly."

Conversation turned to dinner and what on the menu looked better than anything else.

"It all looks delicious," said Sarah.

"Reach out if you need help," Gabby said. "I'm here if there's anything you don't understand."

Sarah looked at her and just beamed. Lisette and Sheridan exchanged a knowing look. At least someone was going to get laid that night.

After they'd ordered, Lisette broached the subject of the map.

"So, library tomorrow morning. What time is your lecture tomorrow?"

"Two o'clock. And I'll need Sarah, unfortunately. We can leave you two at the library though. We have that lecture at two and then an informal question and answer session at three."

"The library doesn't open until ten," Gabby said. "Is it worth it for you guys to come if you've got to be at the university at two?"

"I think so. We may not get much done, but every little bit will help. And Sarah and I really want to help."

"Then it's decided," Lisette said. "I'll text Louis right now and ask him to open the store tomorrow."

"Perfect," Gabby said. "Thank you."

"And I'll swing by the store after dinner to take some pictures of the map for us."

"I'll go with you. For protection of course."

Gabby and Sarah exchanged a knowing look then.

"You're such a gentlewoman." Sarah laughed.

"I try."

They all laughed. Dinner was served and they relaxed into conversations about life in a bookstore versus life as a neurosurgeon.

"You really operate on people's brains?" Gabby said.

"She does," said Sarah.

"But you seem so down-to-earth. I thought surgeons were all egomaniacs."

"You don't know her yet."

"Hey, now!" Sheridan protested to much laughter.

After dinner, Gabby and Sarah climbed into Gabby's car, presumably to take Sarah back to the hotel.

"She'll no doubt take her back to her place. She's very proud of her home," Lisette said.

"Good for her. Sarah will enjoy that, I'm sure. Now, let's get back to the store and get some pictures of the map for tomorrow."

"I hope they'll turn out."

"I'm sure they will."

## CHAPTER EIGHT

L isette turned on the lights inside the bookstore then took Sheridan's hand and walked back to her office. She unlocked the door, let Sheridan in, and locked the door behind them.

"You worried about someone coming in?" Sheridan laughed.

"You never know."

She opened the safe and took the map out while Sheridan turned on the desk lamp. Lisette carefully unfolded the parchment and placed one-third of it on the lampshade.

Sheridan took a picture. Then another. She enlarged the photo and showed it to Lisette.

"What do you think?"

"It'll work. Now let's get some more."

They finished taking pictures of the whole map and Sheridan sent the photos to Lisette's phone and to Sarah's.

"Not that she'll see them tonight."

"You think they're going to sleep together?" Lisette said.

"Why not? They're young. I hope they do, and I hope it's good for both of them."

"I agree."

Lisette placed the map back in the safe and locked it. She stood looking at Sheridan over by her desk. She took off her coat.

"What are you doing? Shouldn't we get out of here?"

"What's the hurry?"

"I guess there isn't any."

Lisette sat on the couch and patted the cushion next to her. "Have a seat," she said.

Sheridan sat at the other end of the couch. This wasn't what Lisette wanted. She was hyper-aroused after having spent so much time with Sheridan. She intended to have Sheridan have her way with her.

She got on her hands and knees and leaned into Sheridan and kissed her. Sheridan kissed her back, almost frantically. Lisette felt Sheridan's desire, her need, in that kiss. Balancing, she took Sheridan's hand and placed it between her legs.

"No." She took her hand away.

"Yes. Please."

"Not yet."

Lisette lay back on the couch, resting her head on the armrest, and placing her calves on Sheridan's shoulders. Sheridan climbed on top of her and kissed her again. Their tongues danced a hormone-induced tango, tumbling over each other, searching, needing.

Lisette hiked her dress up to her waist and wrapped her legs around Sheridan's waist. Sheridan moved her hand to cup an ass cheek.

"Oh, God, Sheridan," breathed Lisette. "I don't want to wait any longer. Please. Don't make me beg."

Sheridan nibbled her way down Lisette's neck and kissed her exposed chest.

"More, please. I need more."

Sheridan reached behind Lisette and unzipped her dress. She pulled one shoulder down and kissed the sensitive skin it exposed. Lisette shuddered at the sheer pleasure of it.

Lisette pulled her other shoulder off and moved her dress down lower to expose her breasts.

"Oh, fuck," said Sheridan. She licked each pale mound then sucked the hard pink nipples into her mouth. One at a time, she sucked and licked. Lisette had her hands in Sheridan's hair, urging her onward.

Sheridan knew what she was doing, Lisette felt her juices pooling and knew she wouldn't stop. Nor would she let Sheridan stop. This was their moment. She placed her hands on Sheridan's shoulders and tried to move her lower.

Sheridan acted like she didn't notice, but Lisette didn't stop. She continued to apply pressure. She unwrapped her legs from Sheridan's waist. She pushed her dress down until she kicked it off. She lay there naked, exposed, and more ready than she'd ever been.

Sheridan ran her hand down over Lisette's hip and down her upper thigh.

"Yes. Dear God, yes," moaned Lisette.

She felt Sheridan's fingertips tracing her inner thigh and almost came at her tenderness. Sheridan gently spread her legs.

"Damn. You're beautiful."

She ran her fingers from Lisette's clit to her center and plunged her fingers inside.

"Oh, God, yes!"

Sheridan lowered her mouth and ran her tongue over Lisette's clit. Lisette was overwhelmed by the feelings Sheridan was coaxing out of her. She arched her back and urged Sheridan to plunge faster and deeper. She placed her hand on the back of Sheridan's head, keeping her right where she was.

She was losing coherent thought. Nothing mattered but the magic Sheridan was working on her body. She felt the heat bubble forming in her belly. She felt it expand. She was so close. The bubble grew and grew until it exploded, shooting white heat throughout her extremities. She finally came back to her body.

"Oh, my God, Sheridan. That was amazing."

"Mm." Sheridan kissed Lisette's inner thighs, her hips, her belly, her chest, and finally her mouth.

"Thank you," Lisette managed.

"It was my pleasure."

"I don't know about that." Lisette laughed, still trying to catch her breath.

They kissed for an eternity. Lisette reached down to unbuckle Sheridan's belt.

"No. Not now. I'm okay for the moment."

"Are you sure?"

"Positive. Let's get out of here."

"Will you stay with me tonight? At my house?"

"I'd love that," said Sheridan.

"Help me get dressed?"

"Gladly."

When Lisette was dressed, she grabbed her purse, and they left the bookstore.

"Are you okay to drive?" said Sheridan.

"I'm fine. I'm very relaxed at the moment."

"I'm glad to hear that."

They held hands as they drove to Lisette's house. Sheridan felt like all was right in her world. Except for the fact she was hornier than hell. She should have let Lisette please her, but she was nervous. She was happy she remembered how to please a woman, but what if she couldn't come? It had never been a problem for her, and she was incredibly primed, but somehow, she was still scared.

Inside Lisette's house, her grandfather clock chimed midnight.

"It's late," Sheridan said. "We should try to get some sleep."

"We should indeed. We have a big day tomorrow."

"That we do."

Lisette led the way to her bedroom. Sheridan took in the king-sized bed with the gold satin comforter. The room was done in golds and light greens. It was welcoming, but she didn't know if she'd be able to sleep. She was way too keyed up.

"I don't sleep in pajamas," said Lisette. "I hope that won't be a problem."

"Definitely not. I sleep naked, too."

"Oh, nice." Lisette grinned at her.

"I take it that gives you ideas?"

"It does indeed. I'll try to behave, but I can't make any promises."

"I don't want you to behave."

"You don't? Are you sure?"

"I'm positive."

"Then let's get naked."

Sheridan stripped and climbed into bed. What if Lisette thought she was too skinny? What if her body turned her off when she saw her naked? She needed to get out of her head, but didn't know how. She pulled the covers up to her chin.

"Are you shy deep down?" said Lisette.

"I don't think so."

"Then let me see you."

Sheridan hoped the panic didn't show in her eyes as Lisette peeled the covers off her. She kept her focus on Lisette's eyes, looking for a clue as to how she was feeling.

"Mon dieu, you're gorgeous," Lisette said.

"You really think so?"

"Oh, damn. Look at your body. It's even hotter than I imagined."

"You're too kind."

"Kindness has nothing to do with it."

Sheridan pulled Lisette to her and kissed her. The longer they kissed, the more aroused she became. Soon, she pushed all doubts out of her mind and allowed herself to just enjoy the ride.

Lisette dragged her hand down and cupped her breast. Sheridan gasped.

"You're perfect," said Lisette.

"Thank you."

"Oh, babe. You're amazing."

Lisette teased Sheridan's nipples until they were standing at attention. As was the nerve center between her legs. Lisette ran her hand lower until it rested between Sheridan's legs. Sheridan spread her legs wide. She ached for Lisette to pleasure her.

Lisette dragged her fingers over every inch between Sheridan's legs.

"Oh," moaned Sheridan.

Lisette rested her fingers on Sheridan's clit then pressed into it and rubbed. Sheridan moved under her, arching to get Lisette to press harder. Lisette obliged and soon Sheridan was lost in the feeling. Never had she felt so good. She needed release so desperately.

Sheridan grabbed Lisette's wrist and guided her to just the right spot. She tiptoed closer and closer to the edge. Suddenly, she shot into orbit, circling the couple on the bed several times before she came back to her body. She was breathing too heavily to say anything. She lay there, eyes closed, chest heaving, smiling.

"You're amazing," Lisette kissed her cheek.

"You are. Damn, woman."

"Will you hold me as we sleep?"

"Nothing would make me happier."

Sheridan woke in the dark and had no idea where she was. She felt the panic well inside her until she made out Lisette sleeping next to her. The previous night came back to her, and she snuggled closer to Lisette with a smile.

She had no idea what time it was, but it didn't matter. All that mattered was that Lisette was lying naked next to her and seeing her exposed breasts and her legs slightly spread, Sheridan lost control.

She reached out and cupped Lisette's full breast. She took her nipple between her thumb and finger and twisted and tugged it. Lisette moaned in her sleep and spread her legs wider.

Sheridan sucked her nipple then, taking half her breast in her mouth with it. She sucked hard, running her tongue over it.

"Mm," said Lisette.

She moved to Lisette's other breast and repeated until Lisette woke up and held her head in place.

"Good morning," said Lisette.

"Mm," Sheridan said.

She kissed down Lisette's soft belly and back up to her breasts. She slid her hand down between Lisette's legs and used her fingers to make Lisette cry out. Innately proud of herself, she kissed Lisette on her mouth.

"I don't have any idea what time it is, but I just had to have you."

"I know what time it is."

"You do?"

"Time for me to make love to you."

"Please do."

It seemed like Lisette moved in slow motion. Sheridan needed her desperately. She wanted to climax as completely as she had the night before. But Lisette didn't seem to be in any hurry.

"Lisette, please. Don't tease me. Take me to heaven. Now."

"Your wish is my command."

She placed her hand between Sheridan's legs.

"Damn. You really are ready."

"Have I ever lied to you?"

Lisette rubbed Sheridan's clit. Over and over and over until Sheridan couldn't think. She could only feel and what she felt was electricity shorting throughout her body. Until it quit shorting and electricity flowed. It coursed through her body, shooting straight out of the nerve center Lisette had so expertly pleased.

"Damn," she breathed. "Just damn."

"You're fun to love."

"As are you. We're quite a pair."

"We're like a couple of teenagers when we're together."

"That's exactly how I feel," said Sheridan.

She noticed a faint light coming in through the gold curtains.

"I'm too excited about today to go back to sleep."

"I hear you," said Lisette. She looked at her phone. "It's almost seven."

"Let's go back to the restaurant we went to last night and get coffee and breakfast."

"Oh, Sheridan. I love the way you think."

## CHAPTER NINE

Ten o'clock arrived, and Sheridan and Lisette walked up the steps leading to Claire-Martin Library on Rue Saint-Jean. They had seen Gabby's truck in the parking lot, so knew the others had arrived.

They walked in the expansive space and found Gabby and Sarah sitting in the foyer. They walked over.

"We've got the lowdown on where old maps of Canada are," said Gabby.

"The whole country?" Lisette said.

"Yep. I'd rather have too much information than not enough."

"Good point," said Sheridan. "Let's get started."

"The librarian said it was in the rear left portion of the library. I've got the codes, but we need to find the section."

"Fair enough."

They headed in the direction the librarian had instructed.

"What are some codes?"

"M467 through M609."

"Here are some Ms," said Sarah.

"Right. Let's follow this row."

It was already ten fifteen by the time they found the maps.

"Let's just kind of dig in," Sheridan said. "I'll take these shelves. You guys split up and claim your shelves. Let's see what we can find."

Sheridan read the spines of the atlases trying to figure out her next steps. She decided the old maps of Quebec would be a good place to start. She took three atlases and placed them on the table behind her.

She looked at the photos on her phone and tried to find similar outlines in the atlases. Nothing matched. She checked the years on the atlas she was staring at: 1657. How old was the parchment they'd found? She had no way of knowing. Could it be three hundred and fifty years old? Not likely. Sure, the lines were faded, but would they even be able to make them out if the parchment was that old?

She closed the book and moved on to the next one. She scoured maps of Quebec from the 1800s. She felt like it should be there, somewhere. If only she looked harder, strained more.

Her phone buzzed. It was a text from Gabby. She'd found something. Sheridan made her way down the aisle and found Lisette and Sarah already with Gabby.

"It's a map of Acadia," Gabby whispered excitedly. "It's from around the time the English banished the Acadians back to France and off to America. Look. Doesn't this look like the map you found?"

They crowded around her, Sheridan leaning over the others to see what had Gabby so pumped. Gabby was tracing the outline of something in the book. It sure looked like the shape they were chasing.

"Can we see where the X is?" said Sheridan.

"I think it's right around here." Gabby drew a small circle on the page.

"This is great. Well done, Gabs," Lisette said.

"Now we just need to find out where that is on a modern map," Sheridan said. "Let's start looking."

"Already on it." Sarah held up a book of Nova Scotia.

"That's a start," said Lisette. "But Acadia also included New Brunswick, Prince Edward Island, and even parts of Quebec."

"You're kidding," said Sarah.

"I'm not."

"Nova Scotia is a great place to start. We'll look at this book. You two go find us some others," Gabby said.

Sheridan followed Lisette down dark aisles of empty bookshelves.

"Where are we going?" Sheridan said.

"Out of the way of prying eyes."

"Why?"

"I'm excited and I want you. Now."

"Are you crazy?" Sheridan chuckled.

"Try me."

Lisette took Sheridan's hand and placed it between her legs. Sheridan was pleased to find no underwear to impede her. Lisette was definitely ready for her, so she slid her fingers inside her. She withdrew them slowly, rubbed her clit, then drove them deep again.

"Holy fuck," Lisette groaned into Sheridan's shoulder.

Encouraged, Sheridan kept doing what she was doing. She could hear the sounds of her fingers penetrating Lisette's wet heat and wondered if anyone else could as well. She finally pressed her fingertips into Lisette's nerve center and rubbed with all her might. She had to wrap her arm around Lisette to keep her from collapsing in a heap.

"Better?" Sheridan whispered.

"Much. Now, I suppose we should look for maps."

"You think?" They laughed together as they found the stacks with current maps on them.

"Here's a book of modern-day Prince Edward Island," said Lisette. "Although, I just have this feeling that's a long shot."

"Regardless, we should take it back. Just in case. Do you see any of New Brunswick?"

"Why aren't you looking?"

"I don't really want to get your essence all over the books."

"Good point." Lisette blushed.

"Thank you."

The four of them eventually checked out the modern-day maps as well as the old atlas Gabby had found. It was time for Sheridan and Sarah to head to the conference.

"You guys should stay and keep looking," said Sarah.

"I'm actually interested in hearing Sheridan speak," said Lisette.

"You are?" Sheridan was more than a little surprised.

"I am."

"I'm quite sure it'll put you right to sleep."

"I doubt that."

"Well, no offense," Gabby said. "But a potential treasure hunt sounds more appealing to me than whatever you're speaking on. I'll take these back to the bookstore and go over them with a fine-tooth comb."

"Okay," said Lisette. "That's settled. We'll see you back at the store in a few hours."

The three of them climbed into Lisette's car and she drove them to the university. They found the lecture hall and Sarah began getting things set up.

"You're going to be bored out of your mind," Sheridan reiterated.

"I'll be watching you. No way that could bore me."

The crowds started filling the hall.

"It's go time," Sheridan said.

"I'll stay up here in the back. I'll leave the better seats for the actual attendees."

At first, Sheridan was a little uncomfortable knowing Lisette was there but soon got into her groove and fascinated the crowd with new developments in the field of neurology and neurosurgery.

The crowd erupted in applause when she finished. Lisette's heart swelled with pride as she watched everyone in the full hall get to their feet. She may not have understood a lot, but it was clear Sheridan was a brilliant, well-received, neurosurgeon.

Sheridan draped her arm over Lisette's shoulder as they walked to the next hall where the Q&A session would take place. Lisette went to the back of the room and helped herself to coffee and a cookie before taking a seat nearby.

The room was packed, and the questions didn't stop until Sarah stood and announced the session was over. A small crowd gathered around Sheridan then and she graciously entertained them until Sarah again interrupted to tell them Dr. Rousseau had another engagement.

The rest of the crowd filed out of the room and Lisette approached Sheridan.

"You are truly a force to be reckoned with," she said.

"How so?" Sheridan smiled at her.

"You are incredibly popular and obviously well-respected. It's an honor to know you and call you friend."

"Is that what you call her?" Sarah winked at Lisette.

"For now. Yes."

They drove back to the store with a stop at the hotel to drop off supplies and for Sheridan to pack her suitcase. She'd decided to stay with Lisette for the duration. Sarah packed her bags, as well, figuring Gabby wouldn't mind if she moved in with her for the rest of the trip.

Back at the store, Gabby was beaming.

"What is it?" said Lisette.

"Sarah was right. We need to head to Nova Scotia. Sooner rather than later." She showed them the bookmarked pages from a couple of atlases. "It appears to be near Halifax, if not in the city itself. It's hard to tell."

Lisette and Sheridan looked over the maps and Lisette had to agree with Gabby. Halifax seemed to be their next destination. But, when to go? And who would go? Her heart sank as she realized Sheridan probably had no desire to travel that far for this treasure hunt.

"So, when do we leave?" Sheridan said.

"Are you serious?" Lisette arched her eyebrows.

"I was wondering the same thing," said Gabby. "We should head east sooner rather than later."

"I think Sheridan and I will go. To scope it out. If we need you guys or if we think we've found the spot, you two can fly out."

"Fuck, man. That's no fair," said Gabby. "After all, we're the ones who found it."

"And I appreciate that. But none of us are made of money and that's a very expensive plane ticket."

"True."

"I'm sure we can find something to do while they gallivant all over." Sarah wrapped her arms around Gabby's neck.

"Mm. Maybe we will." Gabby kissed her.

"Enough, you two," said Lisette. "I need to do my morning things before the day is gone. I'll be in my office."

"I'll go book us flights for tomorrow," said Sheridan.

"Tomorrow?" Lisette didn't try to deny her surprise.

"No time like the present. Gabby should watch you go through your morning routine so she can open for you tomorrow."

"She's covered for me before. But, come on back, Gabs. We'll do a quick review."

She ran through her list of passwords for different programs and reviewed what needed to be done. She was going fast because she wanted, needed to be with Sheridan again. She was like a drug and Lisette the addict.

"Slow down, boss," said Gabby. "I can't type this fast."

"Sorry," said Lisette. "Where did I lose you?"

"With the Mac password?"

They laughed.

"Okay. Let's take it slowly now."

Satisfied that Gabby would be good to go for the next day or two, Lisette locked her office and found Louis at the register.

"Where are Sheridan and Sarah?" she said.

"They split up. Sarah headed to the romances and Sheridan said something about medical journals? Maybe I misunderstood."

Lisette laughed.

"No. I'm quite sure you understood perfectly."

Lisette wandered over to find Sheridan's nose in a journal that claimed to be about neuropsychology.

"Is there anything you won't read?" Lisette said.

"Romance novels." Sheridan laughed.

"What did you find about flights?"

"We leave tomorrow morning around eleven and get to Halifax around four."

"Great. Thank you. What do I owe you?"

"Not a thing," said Sheridan. "Even though I booked business class. I hope you don't mind."

"I appreciate that, Ms. Moneybags. But I need to pay for my ticket."

"I'll tell you what. You buy dinner, okay? I'm famished."

Lisette swatted Sheridan's arm playfully.

"Fine. But I'm going to start keeping track of all the money you spend on me."

"Don't be ridiculous. I'm courting you. I'm supposed to pay good money. Now, drop the subject, please."

"Consider it dropped. What are you in the mood for? For dinner?" She winked.

"Ah, yes. Someplace we don't have to dress for. I don't want to change. I just want to eat."

"I know just the place."

They walked down the street to a restaurant Lisette knew Sheridan would love. The decorations were amazing, as was the overall ambiance. And the food was to die for.

As they enjoyed their dinner, they discussed their upcoming trip to Halifax.

"You're likely to freeze," said Lisette. "Did you happen to bring warmer clothes?"

"I've got jeans and sweaters and a heavy coat. I'll be fine."

"How long are we staying?"

"A couple of days. Long enough to find the magic X."

"Sounds good. I'm excited to go away with you."

"I'm excited, too," said Sheridan. "And speaking of excited, let's finish dinner so I can get you in bed."

## CHAPTER TEN

Sheridan shed her heavy coat as they stepped out of the airport. It was an unseasonably warm, sunny day in Halifax. "So much for freezing here," she said.

"I swear." Lisette laughed. "It's always cold and rainy here."

"Well, they must have heard I was coming."

They hailed a taxi to take them to their Airbnb on the water. The taxi pulled up in front of a blue cottage with a wraparound porch. Sheridan could already tell she'd never want to leave.

"This place is adorable," said Lisette. "Let's get unpacked and explore."

"We can't lose sight of why we're here. We can stow our suitcases, but then we need to find the X on the map."

"I know. And I'm excited to do that. It's just that…well, just smell. That's fresh sea air."

Sheridan had to smile.

"Yes. I smell that. Okay, we can spend a few minutes checking out the neighborhood before we head downtown. Maybe there's a place to eat here. I'm famished."

They dined on lobster tails and sipped wine and discussed their next actions.

"According to the map Sarah and Gabby found, the X should be somewhere on the south end." Sheridan slid the map across the table so Lisette could see.

"Maybe it's in Long Lake Provincial Park."

"Could be. My question is, once we find it, how are we going to dig it up?"

"That's something we haven't even thought about. Who knows how deep it's buried?" said Lisette.

"I'm sure something will come to us."

"I hope so. I mean it could be tricky since we don't even know what we're looking for."

"Very true. We just need to find the X and then we'll decide how to proceed."

They went back to the cottage and changed into cooler clothes before heading back into the city. They had the taxi drop them at the park. They found a picnic table and spread out the map.

"Okay," said Sheridan. "We seem to be inside the magic area. The X looks to be about five hundred yards east."

"We should start walking then."

"You excited?"

"Very. Aren't you?"

"I'm always excited when I'm with you," said Sheridan.

"Well, once we find the long-lost treasure, I'll let you into my hidden treasure."

"I'll hold you to that."

They walked and walked through the park and down toward another stretch of water. There was a gorgeous church there with a tall spire.

"What religion do you suppose that is?" Sheridan said.

"My guess is Catholic. Let's go check it out."

"Indeed. It could actually be our destination." She showed the map to Lisette.

"Oh, yes. It could be! Wouldn't that be amazing?"

It was St. Mary's Cathedral Basilica. They stepped inside and Lisette looked in awe at the stained-glass windows.

"They take your breath away, don't they?" she said.

"They're beautiful, all right. But I'm not a fan of Catholicism."

"No? Because they don't like our type?"

"That's just the tip of the iceberg."

"I wonder when this was built," said Lisette. "Let's find the office and see if we can ask some questions."

"Wait," Sheridan said. "Those look like old-fashioned confessionals back there."

"So?"

"Come here." She took Lisette's hands and hurried into one of the confessionals.

"What are you doing?"

"Sh."

As the door closed behind them, Sheridan pulled Lisette to her and kissed her hard. She pressed her against the wall and slid her hand down her shorts.

"What are you doing?" Lisette repeated.

"What do you think?"

"Sheridan!"

But Sheridan kissed her again, silencing any more protests. Sheridan found Lisette warm and welcoming and in no time, she was as wet as could be. Sheridan slipped her fingers inside and Lisette moaned into her mouth.

"Come for me baby," Sheridan whispered.

"Oh, God."

Sheridan added another finger and drove them as deep as she could in their confines. She withdrew her fingers and found Lisette's clit swollen and throbbing.

"Holy fuck, Sheridan."

"There you go. Let it happen."

"Oh, God. Oh, damn. Oh, fuck. Yes!"

Sheridan kept rubbing her until she was certain Lisette was through.

"That was fun," she said.

"You're insane. I mean, certifiable." Lisette laughed.

"Mm. You weren't complaining."

"No. No, I was not."

The afternoon sun was bright, especially after the dark confessional, and Sheridan blinked several times to clear her vision. They found the office and went in.

A nun in a habit sat behind the desk and seemed surprised to have visitors.

"Good afternoon," she said. "Can I help you?"

Sheridan instinctively put her hands in her pockets. She felt like the whole world could smell Lisette on her.

"We're curious about the cathedral," said Lisette. "Can you tell us when it was built?"

"Construction started in eighteen twenty and was completed in eighteen twenty-nine."

"Thank you," Sheridan said. "That's all we needed to know."

"Of course." The nun smiled.

They walked back to the park and sat on a bench.

"Okay," said Lisette. "We can agree we're looking for something that had to do with Marie Antoinette, right?"

"I'd say that's a safe bet."

"So that means whatever we're looking for would have been buried after her death in the late seventeen hundreds."

"Potentially," Sheridan said.

"What do you mean, potentially?"

"It could have been buried before she died. We don't know what we're looking for, who buried it, or when."

"Well, yes. I see what you're saying. But much of her belongings were dispersed after she was made prisoner. That would have been the late seventeen hundreds. They tried to sneak them to Austria but were unsuccessful. So, my guess is whatever we're looking for belonged to her and somehow ended up buried over here."

"Well, if that's the case—and it does make sense—then it could be buried under this church."

"Exactly," said Lisette. "So how do we find out? We can't exactly dig up the church."

"Let's take the map back inside and see if we can figure out where the X is."

"Can we do it tomorrow? I'm getting hungry again and would love to head back to the cottage."

"Of course. We've got time. And it's not like the church is going anywhere," said Sheridan.

Lisette stood and took Sheridan's hand.

"Come on. Let's get a taxi."

They snuggled together in the back seat of the cab as it drove them back to the Airbnb. They exited the cab and Lisette's stomach growled as delicious scents wafted on the evening air.

"Do you want to go inside first? Or should we just find food?" Sheridan said.

"We need to change. It's getting chilly out here. Then food."

They dressed in long pants and sweaters then wandered in search of dinner.

"Are you in the mood for seafood again?" Lisette said.

"I want a steak, but you can eat all the seafood you want."

"And I will." Lisette laughed.

They came to a restaurant with a shark head above the front door.

"This looks promising," said Sheridan.

"Let's look at the menu." Lisette pointed to the menu posted by the door. "It doesn't look like you'll get a steak here. Shall we keep walking?"

"No. This pepper jelly burger looks good. I'll have that. Come on. Let's get inside."

The patio was closed due to the fact it was October and there weren't many nice days left in the year. They were seated next to the window with a beautiful view of Halifax Harbor.

"This place is so cute," said Lisette.

"You like wood, I've noticed. Like, whenever a place has wood throughout, you really enjoy it. Why don't you have more exposed wood in your house?"

"I guess I never really thought about it. I suppose I could tear up my carpet and have wood floors, but wouldn't they get cold in the winter?"

"Good question. Seems like they would though, right?"

Dinner was served and they ate in comfortable silence. After dinner, they enjoyed cocktails until the view of the harbor had become lights only.

"Let's get home," said Lisette. "I'm about ready for bed."

"Good call."

Sheridan draped her arm around Lisette's shoulders as they walked the few blocks back to their cottage. Lisette felt safe and secure. Sheridan was everything she had ever dreamed of, and she was so glad they'd found each other.

She sighed dreamily as she leaned against Sheridan.

"Is that right?" Sheridan said. "What was that sigh for?"

"Just thinking how I've never been happier."

"I know that feeling, Lisette. I know it well."

Lisette slept late the next morning and woke when Sheridan placed a cup of steaming coffee on her bedside table. She stretched and smiled at Sheridan.

"Mm. Good morning."

"Nice of you to finally wake up."

"What time is it?"

"Just past ten."

"Why did you let me sleep so late?" Lisette said.

"You were sleeping hard. And I figured you needed it. Now cover up or I'm going to climb back into bed with you."

Rather than pulling the covers over her nakedness, Lisette spread her legs.

"See anything you like?"

"You know I do."

"Take me, Sheridan. Please?"

Sheridan knelt on the bed and buried her face between Lisette's legs. Lisette writhed in pleasure, each stroke of Sheridan's tongue taking her closer and closer to lift off.

Lisette placed her hand on the back of Sheridan's head and pressed her face into her. She rode her face up and down until at last she shot into orbit, leaving Sheridan still feasting on her below.

When she came back to rest in her body, she pulled Sheridan to her for a long kiss, enjoying her flavor on Sheridan's tongue.

"Your turn," she whispered.

"No time, I'm afraid. You get showered so we can get our day started."

Lisette pouted, but it didn't seem to have any effect on Sheridan.

"Up you go," Sheridan said.

"Fine."

Lisette took a quick shower and walked into the bedroom to find Sheridan lying on the bed.

"What are you doing?" she said.

"Waiting for you. Why are you still naked?"

"Maybe I want to straddle your face."

"Tempting though that is, you need to get some clothes on so we can head out."

"Fine. So, what's the weather like today?"

"A bit cooler than yesterday so no shorts today."

"Okay. Thanks. Do we have time for breakfast?"

"I should hope so. I'm starving."

"I've got something you could eat," said Lisette.

"I'm well aware."

Lisette dressed in a pair of capris and an orange tunic sweater. She glanced at Sheridan in jeans and a fisherman's sweater.

"Will I be warm enough?"

"Maybe put on a light jacket."

They took a taxi into town again and walked around the neighborhood until they found a restaurant for lunch. While they waited for their meals, they looked at pictures of the original map and compared them to the map of Nova Scotia they had.

"I wish we had measurements," said Lisette. "We don't know how far a kilometer is, a meter, or anything else. How are we supposed to figure out where exactly the X is?"

"We just need to make an educated guess."

"What if we're wrong? What if this isn't even the right place?"

"We can't think like that. We only have a few hours left to determine if whatever it is is buried here. We can't give up."

After lunch, they walked the short distance to the cathedral. As they opened the heavy wooden door, Lisette's heart raced. They could very well find the answer to the riddle in just a few minutes. She could barely breathe from the excitement.

## CHAPTER ELEVEN

They sat together in a pew and stared at the maps.
"I think it's where the altar is," said Sheridan.
"How can you be sure?"

"Look." She turned the map sideways. "Here's the X. It looks like it's right about where the altar is."

"Let's go look around the altar then."

"Right. Come on."

They approached the altar, and Sheridan kept her hearing on alert in case anyone else happened to come into the cathedral. She didn't want trouble. And she was fairly certain a lesbian couple snooping around the altar in a cathedral was begging for trouble.

They stopped at the communion rail and looked at each other.

"Come on." Lisette tugged on her hand. "Let's look."

"Yep. Let's do this."

They walked around the altar, with Sheridan focused on its base, as if she expected to see an opening there with a treasure buried within. Lisette tapped on the sides of the altar, checking to see if it sounded hollow at any point.

Sheridan was on the far side of the altar, on hands and knees, certain she'd see a clue when she heard a voice.

"What do you think you're doing?"

She quickly stood and saw the nun from the office carrying a vase of flowers.

"We're looking for something," Sheridan said lamely.

"Did you lose something? And if you lost it on the altar where you shouldn't have been in the first place, then it's gone for good."

"No, ma'am," Sheridan said. "Look, we can explain."

"You'd better be able to. Come to the office. Now."

Sheridan had heard of scary nuns before but had never experienced one until then. She was terrified of the older woman in the penguin suit. While she truly believed she and Lisette had done nothing wrong, she wasn't so sure the nun would listen, never mind understand.

They were directed to sit in hard wooden chairs. Sheridan sat up straight and tried to appear unintimidated. She hoped it was working.

"You were trespassing," the nun said.

"The cathedral is open to the public."

"Not the altar. And from the looks on your faces when I caught you, you both knew what you were doing was wrong."

"But we have a really good reason," said Lisette.

"I've called the cardinal. When he gets here, you can explain."

Great, they were being passed up the food chain. Sheridan tried to quell the panic rising inside her. She'd never met a cardinal before and didn't have any desire to meet one now. Unfortunately, she wouldn't have a choice.

"I don't think it's necessary to disturb His Eminence," said Lisette. "We really can explain."

"Silence," said the nun. "He's already been disturbed and he's not happy about it."

The door opened and a large older gentleman wearing a black cassock strolled in.

"Are these the two?" he said. He looked at the nun, not even sparing a glance at either of them.

"Yes, sir."

He turned to face them.

"You were attempting to deface my altar?"

"No, sir," said Lisette. "We wouldn't."

"I expected you to say that. Nevertheless, you were caught red-handed. I'm tempted to call the police. You don't look like the run-of-the-mill vandals, but I can't be too careful."

"Your Honor," Sheridan said.

"Eminence. Your Eminence. Not Your Honor," said the cardinal.

"Oh. Sorry." She went on. "Here's the situation. We found a map that we believe shows where something is buried. We believe it has something to do with Marie Antoinette. We believe it was buried before the church was built. And, according to our map, it would be right about where your altar is."

"You have a map." The cardinal arched an eyebrow at her.

"Yes, sir," said Lisette. She handed him the map they had of Halifax.

"This means nothing to me," he said.

Sheridan took out her phone and showed him the picture of the map on the parchment.

"It's the same shape," she said.

"So it is. Where did you find this map?" He pointed to her phone.

"In an old room in the bookstore I own in Quebec City."

"And why do you think it has something to do with Marie Antoinette?"

"We found a locket with a picture of her with the map."

"I don't know," said the cardinal. "It all sounds far-fetched. And it seems like a lot of work to cover for a little vandalism."

"It wasn't vandalism," said Sheridan. "We were just looking to see if there was an opening or a secret compartment."

"Are either of you even Catholic?" he said.

"I was raised Catholic," said Lisette.

He nodded, but didn't say anything. Sheridan, determined to win him over, went on.

"Surely you can understand what we were doing?"

He exhaled heavily.

"Unfortunately, I believe I do. You're in the wrong place though. I assure you nothing was buried anywhere near here. We would have dug it up when we were laying the foundation. So I can assure you, the fact that your map looks like it would lead you to our altar is strictly coincidental. You're both excused. But if we see either one of you around here again, we will notify the police. Do I make myself clear?"

"Yes." Sheridan stood, grateful to be out of the wooden chair. Lisette joined her and they left the office.

"That was a fucking nightmare," said Sheridan.

"Tell me about it."

"He makes a good point, though. Anything buried there would have been dug up when construction started."

"True." Lisette was more disappointed than she wanted Sheridan to know. "So, what now?"

"Back to the library for maps. Somewhere, something is buried, and we need to find out where."

"How long will you help me search?" Lisette held her breath waiting for the answer.

"That's a good question, my dear. I'd like to stick around until we find it, but who knows when that will be?"

"Yes. I get that."

"Hey, babe. Don't sound so defeated. We have time."

"I'm sorry. It's just... Well, I'm really going to miss you when you leave."

"Leaving will be hard for me too," said Sheridan. "But it won't happen for a while, so let's not think about it."

The next afternoon, they were back in Quebec City. It was cool and rainy, and Lisette missed Halifax and being alone with Sheridan. She knew she had to share her with Gabby and Sarah. But she didn't want to. She wanted her all to herself.

"Penny for your thoughts?" Sheridan said Lisette parked at the bookstore.

"They're not worth a penny."

"Sure, they are. Now, come on. You've gone radio silence on me. What are you thinking?"

"Just how nice it was to be away where it was just the two of us. It was very nice, you know? I truly enjoyed it."

"As did I, Lisette. It was magical. Except for the nun and cardinal bit. I could have done without that."

Lisette laughed. Sheridan had a very good point. She could have lived without that, as well.

Gabby and Sarah were behind the counter when they walked in. Their faces lit up.

"What did you find?" Gabby said.

"Nothing," said Sheridan. "Our map led us to a cathedral and the X was where the altar was."

"So, we were searching around the altar for anything that might help and that's when a cranky nun found us and made us explain everything to a cardinal."

"Say what?" Sarah said. "That doesn't sound fun."

"It wasn't. Believe me," said Sheridan.

Gabby burst out laughing.

"Oh, my God. What an experience though. I don't know anybody else who's gotten in trouble from a cardinal before."

"I wouldn't recommend it," Lisette said.

"So how do we know it's not still buried there?" said Gabby.

"Because anything that had been buried there would have been unearthed when they started construction," Sheridan said.

"That makes sense," said Sarah.

"So where does that leave us?" Gabby said.

"Back to the drawing board," said Lisette. "We need to look harder and do more research before we head off on another wild goose chase."

"Makes sense. Outside of the angry cardinal, how was Halifax? Did you freeze your asses off?" Gabby said.

"Actually, it was quite lovely. Warm temperatures and we stayed at a delightful cottage on the water."

"Very nice," said Sarah.

"It was," Sheridan said. "It was a great, if unfruitful, trip."

"Should we head back to the library?" Sarah said.

"We're going to have to. But not today. Let's have a down day today," said Lisette.

"Easy for you to say," said Gabby. "We've had a couple of down days waiting for you to get back."

"If you two want to go back to the library, you're welcome to. I'll have Louis cover the register. Sheridan? Are you going with them?"

"That depends. What are you going to be doing?"

"Just checking the books and making sure everything is in order."

"Everything will be in order," said Gabby. "I took painstaking efforts to make sure everything would be perfect when you got back."

"And I appreciate that. But I would be remiss not to at least double check."

"Maybe I'll just read for a while," said Sheridan. "I'm not really up for the library today."

"Grab a journal and come read in the office," Lisette said.

"Great idea. Good luck, you two. I hope you find something."

"We will," said Gabby. "I just know it."

Lisette watched them set out and then saw Sheridan wander off through the bookstore, but not in the direction of the medical journals. Interesting. She was busy checking Gabby's work when Sheridan entered the office.

Lisette glanced up and her heart leaped at the sight of Sheridan, tall and handsome, dark and alluring. She wanted nothing more than to have Sheridan take her again. Right then. She felt like a teenager with raging hormones. Never had anyone affected her quite like Sheridan had.

"What are you reading?" she said.

"I brought a book on the French Revolution and one on Marie Antoinette."

"Smart woman. You think we'll find the answers in there?"

"I don't know. Probably not. But at least I'll have a better understanding of what happened when back then."

"I could have helped with that," said Lisette.

"I'm sure. But I love to learn, so I thought I'd read these books. I'll read while you work and then I'll buy the books, so we have them with us."

"Thank you, Sheridan."

"For what?"

"For everything."

Sheridan smiled that lazy smile that drove Lisette crazy.

"My pleasure," she said. "Now, are you going to stare at me all day or are you going to work?"

"Fine. I'll work."

"Maybe I'll reward you when you're finished."

"Mm," said Lisette. "I do like the sound of that."

They sat quietly, Lisette at her desk and Sheridan on the couch. It took Lisette longer than it should have to get her work done. She was distracted. By the mysterious X on the map, but mostly by the delicious Sheridan sitting there reading and driving Lisette crazy in the process.

## CHAPTER TWELVE

Sheridan lay next to Lisette and listened to her breathing even out as she fell asleep after a rather intense lovemaking session. While Sheridan was satiated and happy, she still felt restless. When she was certain Lisette was sleeping, Sheridan turned on the lamp on her nightstand and picked up the biography she'd bought.

Marie Antoinette fascinated her. From her early life through her ruling years, right up to her execution. She'd never given the queen a second thought, but now she couldn't learn enough about her. She was happy to learn she was a strong woman and, after reading a little more, found she was rumored to have had a lesbian lover. Sheridan became a true fan. This had been a woman to be reckoned with.

She was reading about Black Jade, Marie Antoinette's perfume, when Lisette stirred. She rolled over and smiled at Sheridan.

"What are you doing?"

"Reading about Marie Antoinette."

"I didn't wear you out earlier?" said Lisette.

"Yes and no. You definitely calmed me considerably, but I started growing restless and decided I wanted to read some more."

"You need to get some sleep, handsome. Morning will be here soon."

"Okay. I'll try to sleep."

"And I'll try to help." Lisette kissed Sheridan hard on her mouth and Sheridan's whole body buzzed anew. Lisette pulled and twisted Sheridan's small nipples, causing excruciating pleasure that radiated through her body until it came to rest in the nerve center between her legs.

Lisette kissed down Sheridan's body until she knelt between her legs. She spread Sheridan's legs wide and simply stared at her.

"Everything okay down there?" Sheridan said.

"I'm simply admiring you. You're perfect." She lowered her head and took Sheridan in her mouth. Sheridan closed her eyes and let herself get lost in the feelings. Damn, Lisette knew how to make her feel good.

She felt Lisette's tongue deep inside her, then circling her clit before she began lapping at her clit like a cat with a bowl of cream. And speaking of cream, Sheridan could feel there was no shortage of it for Lisette to enjoy.

Sheridan lost her ability to think clearly. She felt the ball of white heat forming deep in her gut as Lisette took her closer and closer to the edge. Suddenly, the ball of heat burst open, sending shockwaves coursing through her extremities.

"Damn," Sheridan managed.

"You are sleepy now? Hm?"

"Yes, ma'am. Come here. Let me hold you and let's get some sleep."

Sheridan awoke in an empty bed a few hours later. She rolled over and tried to fall back asleep, but the hint of sunlight through the curtains made her curious about the time.

She checked her phone. It was seven o'clock. She wondered where Lisette was. She got up and found Lisette sitting at the dining room table, coffee in front of her, lost in thought.

"What's on your mind?" Sheridan said.

"Well, it was this whole Marie Antoinette thing, but seeing you naked has my mind on other, happier thoughts. Shall we go back to bed?"

"In a minute." Sheridan laughed. "Let me get a cup of coffee and then you tell me what your thoughts are on Marie Antoinette."

"Are you going to put a robe on?"

"Are you?"

"Okay," said Lisette. "I'll try and concentrate."

Sheridan poured a cup of coffee and sat next to Lisette.

"Why do you look so concerned?"

"What if it doesn't exist? What if we search forever and never find it? And, please be honest, how much longer can you realistically stay and help us search? And Sarah?"

"Wow. That's a lot to be contemplating at this hour. There's no reason to believe we won't find it. I plan on staying here until we do find it. And I don't have an answer for Sarah. Though, with me up here, there isn't much for her to do at home."

"Yes, but she doesn't have your income. She'll need money."

"I suppose that's true. You let Sarah and me work that out."

"Yes, ma'am. But I wish I could be as sure as you. We honestly don't know anything about that map we found. It could just be where someone was meaning to build a house."

"You can't believe that," said Sheridan. "If that was the case, why lock it in that box? And why the locket of Marie Antoinette with it?"

"True."

"Now, come on. We're both naked, so let's not waste this time."

Sheridan stood and pulled Lisette up. Their naked bodies pressed together made her lightheaded. She wanted to consume Lisette completely. She wanted to leave no doubt in her mind that Lisette was hers and hers alone.

They kissed for what seemed an eternity and proof of Sheridan's arousal trickled down her thigh. She reached a hand between them and found Lisette hot and wet and ready as well.

She picked Lisette up and sat her on the table.

"Sheridan!"

"Sh."

She eased Lisette back and stood between her legs. She bent over and suckled at Lisette's full, firm breasts. Lisette moaned her pleasure and Sheridan kissed down her soft belly until she came to the heaven between her legs.

She licked the length of Lisette, plunging her tongue deep inside, sucking on her lips, and finally pulling her clit in her mouth. She continued to tweak Lisette's nipples while her mouth worked its magic.

Lisette cried out loudly as first one and then another orgasm racked her body. She lay there feeling like a wet noodle. Damn, but Sheridan knew what she was doing.

"You okay?" Sheridan said.

"Mm."

"I'm going to go back to bed. Join me when you're able."

When Lisette could finally trust her legs, she climbed off the table and went to the bedroom. There lay Sheridan, softly stroking the tender flesh between her legs.

"Hey, that's mine," said Lisette.

"Just preheating the oven for you." Sheridan laughed.

Lisette lay next to her and buried her fingers inside Sheridan.

"Oh, fuck. Now's good," said Sheridan.

"Why waste time?"

"No pretense. I love it."

Lisette moved her fingers in and out of Sheridan, who arched her back with every thrust to take her deeper. Lisette was only happy to oblige. She slowly dragged her fingers out and pressed them into Sheridan's clit. It was swollen and slick, and Lisette couldn't resist replacing her fingers with her mouth.

Sheridan was delicious and Lisette almost hoped she wouldn't come so she could lap up her flavors forever. Sheridan pressed Lisette's face into her and Lisette thought she was going to suffocate. But what a way to go.

Sheridan finally screamed Lisette's name as she found her release. Lisette smiled to herself, quite proud of the pleasure she'd given Sheridan. She climbed up next to Sheridan and rested her head on Sheridan's chest.

"Thank you," Sheridan finally said.

"It was my pleasure."

"I don't know about that." Sheridan laughed.

"I should shower," said Lisette. "You can sleep a little more. I'll come get you after I've got everything ready at the store. We can go back to the library."

"That sounds nice," Sheridan said. "I'll see you when you get back."

Lisette tore herself away from Sheridan's fit, naked body and took a shower and got ready for her day. It was another cool, rainy day and she dressed in black jeans and a black sweater. She zipped up her black boots, then her coat, and drove to the store.

"You're here early, boss," said Gabby.

"I want to get everything done so we can go to the library. What did you two find yesterday, by the way?"

"To be honest? It appears that Banff National Park is shaped the same as the part of the map. At least the portion around Lake Louise is."

"Really? Banff, huh? I could handle going there." Lisette laughed.

"Right? Maybe take Sarah and me with you this time?"

"Why not? Fine by me."

"Hey, boss?" Gabby grew serious. "How long are Sarah and Sheridan going to be here?"

"I have no idea."

"Surely you've discussed this with Sheridan."

"Yes. But we still don't have a definitive answer."

"I see."

"I think," said Lisette, "that they plan to stay with us until we find whatever we're looking for."

"Maybe Sheridan can, but I think Sarah is worried about money."

"I understand. But I think Sheridan will take care of her."

"Really?" said Gabby.

"I can't promise that. And to be clear, Sheridan didn't say that. It's just the feeling I get."

"I hope you're right."

"I've got to get some work done. I was going to have you call Louis to come in early, but since y'all found something yesterday, maybe we'll just look at what you found."

"Sounds good. I'll be here when you're ready," said Gabby.

"I'd like Sheridan to see it, too, so it'll have to be after I go pick her up."

"Yes, ma'am. You're the boss."

Lisette came out of the office an hour and a half later and found Sheridan talking to Gabby.

"Well, hello there," said Lisette. "I didn't expect to see you here."

"I slept for a little while. Then decided to come here and save you a trip."

"That was nice of you. Have either of you seen Sarah?"

"She's taking advantage of the sun and reading in the park," said Gabby. "Would you like me to text her?"

"Yes, please. Let's talk about what you two found."

Sarah was back in the store twenty minutes later and she showed Lisette and Sheridan the map she and Gabby had found.

"That's amazing," said Sheridan. "And worth the trip. Who wouldn't want to go to Banff?"

"Can we go this time?" said Sarah. "I really want to see Lake Louise. It's on my bucket list."

Sheridan hesitated briefly, then said, "Of course. I'll get us plane tickets. Where do we fly into?"

"I honestly don't know," said Lisette. "Gabby, will you look it up?"

"Looks like we'd fly into Calgary."

"How far is Banff from there?" said Sheridan.

"About one hundred and forty-four kilometers."

"In English?" Sheridan laughed.

"Around ninety miles." Sarah looked up from her phone. "So not bad."

"Not bad at all. Okay. I'll make the reservations. And I'll see about hotels by Lake Louise."

"Oh," said Sarah. "Maybe a cabin?"

"That would be cool," Gabby said.

"We'll see what's available."

"Come on in the office and let's look," Lisette said.

"Sounds good. You two hold down the fort."

"Did you want to use my computer?" Lisette said.

"I've got my phone. I found flights. We can leave tomorrow."

"Wow. So soon?"

"We might as well strike while the iron's hot."

"Mm. And speaking of hot, how about I lock that door and we get naked again?"

"You're incorrigible, Lisette."

Lisette felt the heat creeping up to her cheeks.

"It's the effect you have on me. I'm not normally like this. As a matter of fact, the last time I had sex before you came into my life was longer ago than I care to admit."

"I know that feeling," said Sheridan.

"Do you?"

"Yes. I got burned in college and threw myself into grad school and the rest of my education and then buried myself in my work. I haven't even been on a date in like fifteen or twenty years. Though that's embarrassing to admit."

"Not really. We were saving ourselves for each other."

"I suppose we were."

"I'm so glad you came into my life, Sheridan Rousseau."

"As am I, Lisette Mouton."

"What do you suppose is going to happen after we find the buried treasure?"

"We'll be rich." Sheridan laughed.

"I mean between us, silly."

Sheridan's violet eyes searched Lisette's as if looking for something.

"I wish I had the answer to that."

"Yes. Me, too."

## CHAPTER THIRTEEN

The drive from Calgary was stunning. The mountains and quaint towns they drove through made the ninety-minute drive fly by. As they pulled into the national park, Sheridan asked Lisette to use her phone to figure out where the cabins that she had rented were located.

"Take a right here," Lisette said. She proceeded to guide them along a river until they reached their destination. The cabins Sheridan had rented sat right on the river, just downstream from the highest falls in Canada. It was breathtaking.

They checked in and went to their respective cabins.

"This place is amazing," Lisette said. "I'm in heaven."

"I never took you as an outdoorsy type."

"I don't know that I am." Lisette laughed. "I've been a city girl all my life. But just look around."

They were standing on their deck and Sheridan had to admit, Lisette was right. The blue of the water and the green of the pines made for a spectacular backdrop. It was cold, though, bitter cold.

"I need to get back inside and warm up," Sheridan said.

"Don't you want to go exploring?"

"Can't we save that for when we get to Lake Louise?"

"Fine. I'll see if the girls want to go exploring," said Lisette.

"Okay. Truth is, I'd love to have a look around. Let me get a coat."

They followed the river up to the falls and watched the powerful current coursing over the rocks.

"I wonder how old these falls are," Sheridan said. Lisette pulled out her phone.

"I can't find an answer to that. It says the first settlers here were in seventeen eighty-eight, but I can't find how old they think these are."

"Thanks for checking, babe."

"Apparently there's a glacier with the same name that is believed to be ten thousand years old. How impressive is that?"

"Very."

They hiked around a little more but soon Sheridan was frozen solid.

"You ready to get Sarah and Gabby and get some dinner?"

"Sure. Thanks for hiking with me. I really enjoyed it."

"As did I. It's gorgeous out here."

"Maybe when we get back to the cabin, we can warm each other up before dinner?" said Lisette.

"I'm always up for that."

It took them a half hour to get back and Sheridan couldn't feel her feet by the time they reached the cabin.

"First things first," she said. "I'm making a fire."

"Oh, excellent idea."

The blaze was roaring, and Sheridan sat on the leather couch with Lisette to watch it burn. There was something mesmerizingly peaceful about a real fire in a stone fireplace. And being in a cabin in the middle of Banff National Park only added to the peacefulness.

Lisette burrowed against Sheridan who draped an arm over her shoulders.

"You cold?" Sheridan said.

"I'm warming up."

"Good."

The scent of Lisette's shampoo wafted up to Sheridan. It caused an animalistic reaction in her. It hinted at vanilla and lavender. It was faint but alluring. She didn't want to simply snuggle with Lisette. She wanted to claim her.

She placed her finger under Lisette's chin and made her look into her eyes. She let her gaze dip to Lisette's full, parted lips. She bent to taste them. The kiss soon morphed into a desire Sheridan had become all too familiar with since spending time with Lisette.

Sheridan eased Lisette back on the couch until she was laying on top of her. She ran her fingers up her sides until she closed her hand on one of her breasts. Lisette moaned into Sheridan's mouth. Sheridan brought her knee up and pressed it into Lisette's center while she kissed her and fondled her.

Soon, she needed more. She fumbled with the button and zipper on Lisette's jeans, searching for the paradise she knew she'd find. She slid her hand inside and found Lisette hot and wet. She almost lost her head she needed Lisette so badly.

"You guys decent?" There was a pounding on the door. "We're ready for dinner. Are you coming?"

"Well, I was about to," Lisette whispered.

"Give us a second," Sheridan called back. She sat up. "Shit."

"Tell me."

They got themselves together, put on their coats, and went out to join the others.

"What took you so long?" Gabby said. "I thought I was joking when I asked if you were decent."

"Very funny," Lisette said. "We were just dozing on the couch."

"Yeah. I bet."

They had dinner in a huge cedar cabin with a view of the river. The food was delicious, and the company was wonderful.

"So, Lake Louise tomorrow, huh?" said Sarah.

"Indeed," said Sheridan. "Let's go back to our cabin and review the map again to see if we can figure out exactly where the X is."

They went back to their cabin and did their best to decipher the maps. They placed the picture of the original parchment next to the map of Lake Louise Gabby had found. But it didn't help. The parchment photo was faded and no matter how big they enlarged it they couldn't determine what exactly they were looking at.

"The best I can tell, we need to be on the south side of the lake," said Sheridan. "Once there, we'll have to try to decipher these again."

"I agree," said Lisette. "We want to be on the south side."

The next morning, they stopped at a general store and bought shovels.

"We need to be careful, though," said Gabby. "We don't want to ruin the pristine beauty."

"You're correct," said Lisette. "No digging unless we're absolutely certain."

Lisette was thoroughly enjoying this adventure, even with the coitus interruptus from the previous evening. Sheridan had more than made up for it after dinner.

"Oh, my God," exclaimed Sarah from the back seat. "It's gorgeous."

"It truly is," said Lisette.

"Okay, so from what I saw," Sheridan said, "the only place to park is at the Upper Lake Louise parking area. So, we'll have to hike down to the south side."

"We can do that. No problem," Gabby said.

"Even carrying shovels shouldn't be a problem," said Sarah. "It looks like pretty flat terrain around the lake itself."

"Maybe we should leave the shovels in the car first," Lisette said. "We can always come back and get them."

"I agree," said Sheridan.

Sheridan parked the car and took Lisette's hand as they started out on the trail. Lisette was in heaven. The lake was beyond gorgeous, and she was there with Sheridan. Life couldn't possibly get any better. Unless, of course, they found the treasure.

It took about forty-five minutes for them to reach the south side, and they found some large rocks where they could view the maps.

"I don't know," said Lisette. "It looks like the X is in the middle of the lake."

"That can't be," said Sarah. "Let me look closer."

"She may be right." Gabby moved out of the way and let Sarah see.

Sheridan pointed to the X on the picture of the parchment and then held up the map for herself and Sarah to study.

"Ugh," Sarah said. "So, this was a wasted trip?"

"Oh, ye of little faith," said Sheridan. "Let's walk a little north and double check."

They backtracked a bit and shifted the position of the map. Try as they might, the X was always in the middle of the lake.

"Damn," Sheridan said. "Okay. That's two failed trips. Next time, we do more research before we set off."

"It wasn't a completely failed trip," said Sarah.

"No?" Gabby said.

"No. We got to see the majestic Banff National Park and stood at the edge of the gorgeous Lake Louise. I never would have done these things if we hadn't been on this treasure hunt."

"You are quite right," said Lisette. "It was a wonderful break from the day-to-day and I am immensely grateful we came."

"I like the way you think." Sheridan kissed her and Lisette went weak in the knees. Just a peck from Sheridan had that effect on her. She had it bad and she knew it. How long would it last though? How would she be able to go on when Sheridan finally went back to the States? She honestly didn't know.

"Let's hike around the whole lake," Sarah said. "I mean, we're here. Why not?"

Sheridan stashed the map in her backpack and slid her phone into her pocket. Lisette took her hand, and they started hiking around the lake. It was a chilly October day and the breeze off the lake was crisp indeed.

Lisette felt alive and invigorated. The tall pines surrounded them, and the blue of the lake soothed her. And Sheridan's grip on her hand warmed her insides. All of them. Her thoughts left the beautiful scenery and fast-forwarded to what she hoped would happen in the privacy of their cabin when they returned.

Lisette was an icicle by the time they reached the car.

"Let me in. I'm freezing," she said.

"Door's unlocked. Climb in." Sheridan laughed.

"Oh, my God, I'm cold."

"Here." Sheridan cranked the heat. "This should help."

"Oh, thank you."

"Is there a back seat heater?" said Sarah.

"Never mind. I found it," Gabby said.

"Okay," said Sheridan. "Is everyone comfortable? Shall we head back to the cabins?"

"Yes, please," Lisette said.

Lisette was lost in thought on the drive back. She needed to come up with a way to make Sheridan stay. She couldn't bear the thought of her leaving. She also couldn't believe they'd only known each other a couple of weeks. It seemed like they'd been together forever. Sheridan was her one and only. She knew it in her heart. How did Sheridan feel though? Lisette knew she'd have to ask to know for sure.

Sheridan pulled into the parking spot in front of their cabin.

"Lunch, then exploring?" said Gabby.

"Lunch, then warmth. I think I'd like to read in front of the fire," Lisette said.

"You can do that at the bookstore."

"Give me an hour and then I'll be ready to explore some more. I need warmth first though."

After lunch, Gabby and Sarah waved good-bye to Lisette and Sheridan as they set out on the hiking trail. Lisette watched as Sheridan built a roaring fire in their cabin.

"Would you mind getting my book out of my suitcase?" Lisette said.

"Sure thing. You get comfy. I'll be right back."

When Sheridan disappeared into their bedroom, Lisette stripped. She lay on the bearskin rug and spread her legs wide, so Sheridan could have no doubt about what she wanted.

"Oh, fuck," said Sheridan. "Damn, but you're beautiful."

"See anything that interests you?"

"Everything. Every fucking inch."

"Come and take it."

Sheridan quickly undressed and lay on top of Lisette. The feel of their skin against each other made Lisette dizzy with need. She had to have Sheridan take her every which way. No one made her feel like Sheridan did. No one ever had.

Lisette kissed Sheridan and all thoughts flew from her mind. She could only feel. And she felt Sheridan's strong, skilled fingers spreading her lower lips and entering her. Lisette spread her legs wider and arched up to take Sheridan deeper and deeper. She needed more, but didn't know how to let Sheridan know.

She reached her hand down between them and found her clit slick and swollen. While Sheridan continued plunging her fingers, Lisette rubbed her clit until she cried out and rode wave after wave of her climax.

Lisette flipped around so her face was buried between Sheridan's legs and Sheridan's tongue easily found her center. Lisette focused on pleasing Sheridan, wanting to give her all the pleasure she'd received from her. She closed her lips around Sheridan's throbbing nerve center and licked and sucked until Sheridan let out a guttural moan, just before she sent Lisette into orbit yet again.

## CHAPTER FOURTEEN

Back in Quebec City, things settled into a nice routine. Sarah and Sheridan spent hours at the library searching for maps. When they found one that looked promising, they took it back to Lisette's office and pulled up the modern-day version of the map to see if it might be plausible.

After a few days of this, they were rapidly losing hope of ever finding the mysterious X.

"Dr. Rousseau, may I ask you a question?" Sarah asked one day in the library.

"Go for it."

"I don't know how to say this exactly." Sheridan glanced up at her and saw tears in her assistant's eyes.

"Sarah? What's wrong?"

"I'm sorry, ma'am, but I'm running out of money."

"You are?"

"Yes. I paid my bills today and I had to dip into my savings."

"That's not good," Sheridan said.

"I'm afraid I need to go home and go back to work. But, with you here, I don't really have a job." Sarah was sobbing.

"Sh. Come here." Sheridan took her in her arms. "I'll PayPal you some money. I can do that. Would that help?"

"I can't take your money."

"You do all the time. You're still my assistant. Even here. So, I'll pay you for that. Just tell me how much I owe you. I don't have anything to do with payroll, so I have no idea how much you make."

"Just enough to cover the next two weeks, okay?" said Sarah.

"At least. I'll send more if we're here much longer."

"Thank you so much, Dr. Rousseau."

"It's my pleasure."

That evening, Sheridan was fixing dinner for herself and Lisette.

"I had an interesting conversation with Sarah today," she said.

"Really? What about?"

"Our extended stay here is killing her financially."

"I'm sorry to hear that," said Lisette. "Will she have to go back?"

"Well, she should. But she works for me. And if I'm not there, there's no work for her."

"Oh, Sheridan, no. I don't want to hear this. Please say you're not leaving me. Not yet. I'm not ready."

"We have a couple more weeks. But then, I have to think of that poor kid. She needs to work."

"I can hire her at the bookstore. That way she can work and make money."

"That's very kind of you," said Sheridan. "But I don't think she has the paperwork necessary to work in this country. And I'm not sure you'd pay her quite what she makes working for me."

"Try me," Lisette said. "I do quite well, you know."

"I don't doubt that. I didn't mean to imply anything to the contrary. It's just, well, as a neurosurgeon, I bring in a lot of money."

"And you pay your assistant accordingly?"

"Apparently so," Sheridan said. "I was surprised how well we pay her."

"Well, that makes me happy. But, Sheridan. Two more weeks? Only? That's not enough time."

"I know, babe. I've been thinking."

"Yes?"

"To be honest, so far, I've come up empty. We just need to prepare ourselves, I guess."

For the second time that day, Sheridan looked into the teary eyes of a woman she cared about.

"Please don't cry," she said.

"I really like you."

"And I really like you. Please. We've got a couple of weeks left. Let's not spend them being miserable. Shit! Dinner's burning."

"Let's go out. I need to get out of this house right now anyway. I feel very claustrophobic."

"Okay. I'll get our coats."

Sheridan hailed a taxi so they could both enjoy wine with dinner. At the restaurant, she looked into Lisette's chocolate eyes.

"Are you okay?"

"I may have to move."

"What? Why?"

"I don't want to live with your memory haunting me every time I turn around."

"Babe," Sheridan said. "You're getting way ahead of yourself. Let's see what happens. In the next two weeks, we may find a buried treasure and none of us will ever have to work again."

Lisette smiled through her tears.

"I hope you're right."

"Me, too."

After dinner, they went for a moonlit stroll to check out Halloween decorations. Quebec City was all decked out for the upcoming holiday. City hall was decorated with spiders, pumpkins, and scarecrows. There was a festive feeling in the air.

"I've always loved Halloween," said Lisette. "It brings the city together. Or so it feels."

"Do they trick-or-treat here?"

"They sure do."

"We need to decorate your house, then. We only have a couple of days."

"No need," said Lisette. "We'll give out candy at the store. The kids love going down Rue Ste-Jean."

"I'm sure. How fun. I'm glad I'll be here to participate."

"Me, too, Sheridan. Everything is better when you're involved."

"You're too kind."

"I'm honest."

Sheridan stared into Lisette's eyes, which spoke volumes. Everything they hadn't found the words for screamed at Sheridan from Lisette's eyes. Sheridan looked away. She still didn't want to put anything in words. She didn't want to jinx what they had by putting expectations on it. She wrapped her arm around Lisette and pulled her close.

"So, we'll decorate the store tomorrow?" she said.

"We will indeed. Gabby loves decorating. As do I. I'm glad you enjoy it too."

"Very much. I'll miss the trick-or-treaters back home, so I'm glad we'll have some here."

"It will be a late night at the store on Halloween. People come by until ten or so."

"That late?"

"Oui. Adults come by for hot chocolate or hot apple cider. Halloween is a big deal here."

"Most excellent."

The next morning, Sheridan helped Lisette load boxes of decorations into the car to take to the store.

"Why don't you just keep these at the store?" she said.

"There's no room."

"You have the secret room downstairs. You could use that."

"Oh, yes. I suppose we could."

Gabby and Sarah put decals on windows while Sheridan hung spiderwebs from the ceiling. Lisette was in her office balancing the books. She was sad she was missing the fun, but knew there would be more fun to be had. She had to get her work done first.

As she logged out of her QuickBooks app, she took a moment to contemplate what she was doing with Sheridan. She was falling hard for her. That much she knew. But why? How could she have all these intense feelings for someone she really barely knew? And, again, how would she go on when Sheridan left?

She supposed they could maintain a long-distance relationship. It wasn't something she'd ever considered. She'd heard of them and had always thought they weren't for her, but perhaps she'd judged too quickly. Would she be willing to do that with Sheridan? She was getting ahead of herself. Was that something Sheridan would even be interested in?

Lisette let out a heavy sigh. She had far more questions than answers. She needed to let them all go for now and help with decorating for her favorite holiday. She found most of the boxes empty when she joined the others.

"You've been busy," she said.

"We have." Sheridan kissed her. "Did you get everything done?"

"I did." She opened up a box filled with small jack-o-lanterns. She carried them around, placing them on tables throughout the store. She came back to get more and found Sheridan decorating the cash register with spider webs.

"That looks amazing," said Lisette. "I'm so glad you love Halloween."

"I do. And I'm like a little kid decorating. I'm having the time of my life."

"It's my absolute favorite holiday."

"Is that right? It ranks up there for me. But I'm a sucker for Christmas. The lights, the peace on earth bit. Exchanging presents. I love it."

"Peace on earth, eh?"

"Mm."

"I wish for that every day," said Lisette.

"As do I." Sheridan kissed Lisette again. Lisette stood on her tip toes and pressed herself against Sheridan. Sheridan wrapped her arms around Lisette and held her close. Their kiss deepened and Sheridan finally pulled away, breathing heavily.

"Come to my office," Lisette said.

"Gladly."

Lisette locked the door behind them and stepped back into Sheridan's arms. Sheridan kissed her hard on her mouth, then nibbled and sucked down her neck.

"Don't you dare mark me." Lisette laughed.

"I'll wait and mark your inner thighs."

"Please?"

Sheridan lifted Lisette's sweater over her head and unhooked her bra. She bent to take a hardened nipple in her mouth while she unzipped Lisette's slacks. She kissed down Lisette's belly until she was kneeling between her legs. She pulled Lisette's pants down just far enough to be able to feast on her.

Lisette balanced herself by holding on to Sheridan's strong shoulders. She gyrated her hips into Sheridan's face, feeling nasty and depraved. And she liked it. She wanted to feel Sheridan's tongue everywhere. And she did.

Sheridan sucked on Lisette's lower lips, causing Lisette to moan in ecstasy. No matter what Sheridan did or how she did it, Lisette always felt such joy and pleasure from her.

Her legs were quivering, and she knew she was close. Sheridan knew what she was doing, and Lisette knew the release she was about to feel would far surpass any release she'd ever experienced.

"Hey, boss?" Gabby called.

"No," Lisette breathed.

"You in there?"

Lisette struggled to calm her voice.

"I'll be right out."

And then Sheridan did it. Whatever she did. It didn't matter, but Lisette catapulted out of her body and into another atmosphere.

"Mon dieu," Lisette whispered. "Oh, my God what you do to me."

"Mm. That was fun."

"I'm sorry I can't repay you."

"You will. Now get yourself together. Your public awaits. I need to wash up."

"Use my bathroom."

"Okay. You all right?"

"I am," said Lisette. "Let me go see what the emergency is."

There was no emergency, though. Gabby just wanted to ask if she and Sarah could go buy a few more decorations.

"I think we need scarecrows. And witches."

"I think you're right. Here's the store card. Go crazy." Lisette laughed.

"Can we trust you two here alone?" said Gabby.

"Of course. Louis is here somewhere too. Hurry back."

Lisette heard her office door closed and turned to see Sheridan standing there with a smug smirk on her face. Lisette crossed over to her.

"You look rather proud of yourself."

"I am. It's not every day I get to get on my knees and worship at your altar with a store full of people on the other side of the door."

Lisette blushed.

"Well, when you put it that way."

Sheridan kissed her.

"You're going to get me worked up again," Lisette said.

"No complaints here."

"Very funny."

Lisette found Louis and asked him to watch the register while she and Sheridan took the boxes into her office.

"I don't understand why we don't put them downstairs," Sheridan said again.

"It's always kind of felt off limits down there."

"It shouldn't anymore. It's got plenty of space. You should definitely use it for storage."

"Okay. Let's carry these boxes down there."

"Be careful on the stairs. I don't want you getting hurt."

"I'll be careful."

Lisette walked down first and set her boxes in a corner. She turned on the desk lamp for Sheridan who was right behind her. Once all the boxes were situated, Lisette suggested they head back up.

"Not so fast. I've never really looked around down here," Sheridan said. "Give me a minute to check out the paintings and things."

Lisette sat at the desk and watched Sheridan study the paintings. She snuck up behind Sheridan as she gazed at one painting of the French Revolution.

"What do you think?"

"Fascinating. So much death and despair."

"Let's get your mind on something besides that." Lisette reached around and unbuttoned Sheridan's fly.

"I thought this place was off limits?"

"Is what's in your jeans off limits?"

"Not to you. Never to you," said Sheridan.

She turned around to give Lisette easier access. It was over too soon. Sheridan tried to hold off, but the sight of Lisette, the sweet and proper Lisette, with her hand down Sheridan's jeans in the secret room of the bookstore was too much. Sheridan cried out Lisette's name and Lisette beamed with pride. She loved making Sheridan feel good.

## Chapter Fifteen

Halloween dawned dark and rainy. Sheridan woke alone in bed. It was pitch-black in Lisette's room and the sound of the rain pelting the windows made her snuggle further under the covers.

"Babe?" she called.

"Good morning." Lisette walked into the room carrying two steaming cups of coffee.

"Holy shit." Sheridan took in Lisette's costume. She was the sexiest witch Sheridan had ever laid eyes on. From the tips of her stiletto heels, up her fishnet stockings, to the hem of her oh-so-short skirt, to the low dipped bodice, to the tip of her pointed hat.

"You need to come back to bed. Now."

"I can't, sweetheart. I'm all dressed up."

"No. You can get dressed again. I'm on fire. I need you now."

"Hold that thought until tonight," said Lisette.

"I can't. Holy shit. I'm so turned on right now."

"Show me?"

"Get undressed."

"No." Lisette pulled the covers off Sheridan. "Your nipples are hard."

"Of course they're hard. Have you looked at you?"

Lisette spread Sheridan's legs.

"Oh, my. You're swollen and glistening. When was the last time you were pleased by a witch?"

"Never."

"There's a first time for everything," Lisette said.

Lisette slid her fingers between Sheridan's legs. She felt so good as she stroked all Sheridan's hot spots.

"Listen to how wet you are," said Lisette.

"Oh, God, you feel good."

Lisette withdrew her fingers and pressed into Sheridan's clit. She rubbed it and circled it and rubbed it some more until Sheridan screamed her release. Lisette sucked Sheridan's juices off her fingers.

"Oh, fuck. You're getting me hot again."

"You just relax, stud. We'll have time tonight. But I need to get to work."

"It's awfully early still, isn't it?"

"There's a meeting at city hall for all business owners to go over our plans for keeping the city safe tonight. I have to go."

"Fine," Sheridan said. "Duty calls. But know every second I spend with you I'm going to want to be fucking you."

"Fair enough." Lisette kissed Sheridan and left the room.

Sheridan heard the front door close. Damn. It was going to be a long, frustrating day. She checked her phone. Seven thirty. She rolled over and fell back asleep.

When she woke again, it was a little lighter, but not much. Her phone said it was nine o'clock, so she decided to get up. She nuked the coffee Lisette had brought her earlier and sat sipping it, trying to decide what she wanted to dress up as for the day. She had no costume with her, obviously, so she would have to go buy one. She only hoped every place wasn't sold out.

It was then she saw the clothing bag on the other dining room chair. There was a note on it.

*I guessed at the size. I hope it fits. See you soon, xx.*

She opened the bag and found an old-fashioned vampire costume. It had dark slacks, a white shirt, a cane, a cape, and a top hat. Sheridan was very excited. She took a nice, hot shower and dressed in her costume. She had black dress shoes that went extremely well with the costume.

She checked herself out in the mirror and was happy with her reflection. Everything fit perfectly and she looked sharp. No pun intended. She snickered to herself, put in her fangs, and hailed a taxi.

Sheridan looked around for Lisette as she entered the bookstore. She was nowhere to be seen. She wandered back to the register where Louis stood, also dressed as a vampire.

"Hey, Louis. Have you seen Lisette?"

"She went out to get more donuts and cider. She should be back soon. You look amazing, by the way."

"Thank you! As do you."

"Oui. You need a little blood coming out of your mouth, though. Here."

He handed her a little red ampule and she squeezed enough to look like a trickle of blood was coming from the corner of her mouth.

"Much better," said Louis.

"Thanks."

Sheridan wandered to the medical section of the store and sat down to read a new journal that had just come out. She wasn't able to see the front door from where she sat, but figured Louis would tell Lisette she was there.

Sure enough, Lisette approached her about a half hour later.

"You look stunning," Lisette said.

"And you look devourable."

"Still?"

"Always. Shall we go into your office and let me have my way with you?"

"You are naughty. And no. I told you. Tonight."

"I don't want to wait," said Sheridan.

"I'm not about to take off my costume and then put it back on. It's not an easy costume to get into."

"Oh, babe. You can wear that costume. I'll make my way around it. Or under it."

Lisette playfully slapped Sheridan on the shoulder. But she had to admit, the concept of Sheridan's head under her skirt appealed to her in ways she hadn't expected.

"Come have some cider. And a doughnut or two. They're wicked good."

"Gladly. You lead the way."

Lisette could feel Sheridan's gaze burning into her hips so gave an extra sway or two on the way to the register.

"You are pure evil," Sheridan growled.

Lisette simply laughed. When they got to the counter, there were a dozen people there helping themselves to the treats.

"I'm glad we have plenty of goodies," said Lisette.

"Speaking of goodies, can we go to your office?"

"Patience, my dear."

She handed Sheridan two apple cider doughnuts and a cup of hot apple cider.

"Damn." Sheridan took a bite. "That's really good. Where did you find them?"

"A bakery up the street makes them every year. I agree. They're to die for."

"We should have made some mulled wine," Sheridan said.

"Sorry. This is a family event. No alcohol."

"Gotcha."

"I'm about exhausted from smiling. Let's go into my office so I can relax."

"Now you're talking," said Sheridan.

Lisette really just wanted to put her feet up and be out of the public eye for a moment. She didn't mean to lead Sheridan on, but she really just needed to be for a few minutes.

She sat in her desk chair and put her feet on her desk.

"Much better." She kicked off her shoes.

"Oh, no. Keep the shoes on."

"No. They're killing my feet," said Lisette.

"Fine. How about you rest your legs over my shoulders?"

"You don't stop, do you?" But she was laughing.

"Holy shit, babe. You are dressed like that, and I've kept my hands and mouth to myself. I'm only human though."

"You do look quite dapper in that outfit. But lose the fangs, please."

Sheridan quickly took out her fangs and set them on Lisette's desk. She set her hat down, too. She got on her knees and coaxed Lisette's legs off the desk and over her shoulders. Lisette felt wanton as she watched Sheridan's head disappear under her skirt. Sheridan pulled Lisette's crotch to the side and licked the length of her.

"Oh," Lisette moaned. "Oh, yes."

"Mm."

Sheridan had a magical tongue, and she kept getting Lisette more and more aroused. Lisette leaned her head back and closed her eyes, but half the fun was watching Sheridan's head bobbing under her skirt. Soon, it didn't matter. Lisette couldn't keep her eyes open any more. She squeezed them shut and watched the light show burst forth in her eyelids and Sheridan finally took her over the edge.

"Thank you," said Sheridan.

"Thank you." Lisette laughed.

"I wish I had a strap-on with me."

Lisette widened her eyes. She'd heard of those, obviously, but had never actually seen one.

"Why?"

"So I could take you standing up. I'd love to press you against the wall and slide inside you while watching your bare chest heave."

"My chest is not bare."

"It may as well be."

"You've got quite an imagination," Lisette said.

"*Oui*." Sheridan laughed.

"Oui indeed."

The rest of the day passed with more people milling about inside the store. Several bought books, but many just came to socialize.

"You should go check out the other businesses in the area," Lisette said.

"Come with?"

"I don't know if I can get away."

"Well, those doughnuts were good, but I need a meal. I don't mind eating by myself, but I'd love for you to join me."

"Why not? I'm hungry too. Let's go."

They grabbed their coats, and Sheridan opened the umbrella and held it over both of them. Lisette snuggled close to Sheridan as they walked and braced herself against the wind that was blowing the rain in under the umbrella.

They ducked into the first café they came to. The smell of warm cider drifted on the air, as well as the scent of freshly baked bread.

"Let's get a table," Sheridan said.

They ordered lunch and ate it in companionable silence. Lisette would glance at Sheridan periodically, still unable to believe someone as gorgeous would be with her.

"Everything okay?" Sheridan said.

"Everything is better than okay. You do make a striking vampire."

"Why thank you. And you make a delicious witch."

Lisette felt the heat creep up her chest and flood her cheeks. She glanced around to make sure no one had overheard.

"What are you worried about?" Sheridan said.

"What do you think?" Lisette stage-whispered.

"No one heard me. Your status among the Quebec City Chamber of Commerce is secure."

"You're so funny."

"Does Quebec City have a chamber of commerce? Do you even know what one is?"

"Yes and yes." Lisette laughed. "And I am a member."

"Why doesn't that surprise me?"

"It shouldn't."

"Have you ever thought about running for office?" said Sheridan.

"Why?"

"I don't know. You're a business owner. And a popular one at that. You could control what goes on in your quaint city."

"Thanks, but no."

"I think you should."

Lisette listened to Sheridan's words but tried to read between the lines. If Lisette held office, she'd be entrenched here. Was that what Sheridan wanted? For Lisette to be firmly here so that she couldn't move to the States with Sheridan? Or was Sheridan thinking of moving to Quebec City? The thought warmed her cockles. Sheridan moving here would please Lisette no end.

"Wow," Sheridan said. "I was half-joking, but you just went off in space. Are you considering it?"

"I don't know. Maybe."

"Right on. Okay. Let's get back to the store."

The afternoon passed quickly with more people coming and going. But as soon as the sun went down, that's when the fun started. Lisette stood at the counter with Sheridan and handed out candy to little ghouls and goblins. There were superheroes and princesses, miniature vampires, and the occasional ghost.

Lisette had never been happier. She loved this holiday and loved her city. And sharing it all with Sheridan? Priceless.

## CHAPTER SIXTEEN

G uilt had been gnawing at Sheridan. Ever since Sarah had pointed out she needed money. Sheridan and Sarah had lives back in the States. Sarah depended on Sheridan for her job. Others depended on Sheridan for their lives. And here she was on essentially an extended holiday.

But the treasure. That always shook her out of her reverie. She needed to quit worrying and focus harder. Once they found the treasure... What? What would happen then? Would Lisette be willing to give up her beloved city? The place she was born and raised, as were generations of her family before her?

How did she really feel about Sheridan? That question scared her enough to make her change her line of thinking. She needed to get to the library and study more maps.

"Hey, sweetheart," said Lisette. "What's on your mind?"

"Nothing. Why?"

"You looked deep in thought."

"I just feel like we're missing something."

"What?" said Lisette.

"The map. The treasure. I feel like it shouldn't be this hard."

"If it wasn't this hard then anyone could have found it."

"As if anyone knew there was a secret map locked in a box in your hidden room?"

"True."

"I'm heading to the library. I'll text Sarah to meet me there. Maybe today will be the day we figure things out," Sheridan said.

"Well, if you don't, I hope you don't get discouraged."

Sheridan looked at Lisette. She had words she wanted to say. Words she needed to say. Yet she swallowed them.

"I'll see you at the bookstore a little later," she said.

"Don't I get a kiss good-bye?"

"Of course." But it was a chaste kiss. She couldn't give more at the moment.

The library was becoming her enemy. It contained secrets she needed, but it didn't show them to her. She struggled to work up excitement to look over map after map, but nothing jumped out at her.

"Hey, Dr. Rousseau," Sarah said. "Having any luck?"

"No."

"I don't mean to be a Debbie Downer, but how long are we staying here? I mean, when do we give up and go home? I miss home."

"I know. I feel that way, too. I honestly don't know how much longer we can stay here. It's been fun, but our lives have been on hold long enough."

"Does that mean we're going back to Houston?"

"I feel like we should. On the other hand, damn, I hate giving up."

Sarah laughed.

"Not giving up is what's made you one of the top neurosurgeons in the country, in the continent even."

"Thank you for that. I feel like if we leave, we let Lisette and Gabby down. If we stay, we let our patients down."

"It's a tough spot to be in," said Sarah. "Maybe you could convince Lisette to move to Houston? Or at least come back with us and check it out."

"I'd love that. But she's got her bookstore here."

"Houston could always use a new bookstore."

"Good point," said Sheridan.

They looked over maps until early afternoon when Sheridan took Sarah to lunch before they made their way back to the bookstore. Lisette was nowhere to be seen.

"Is she in her office?" Sheridan asked Gabby.

"I think so. She's been in there since early this morning if she is. I mean, I haven't seen her come out."

Sheridan texted Lisette to ask where she was. Lisette opened the office door a few minutes later.

"Hey, you two. I'm glad you're here. Sheridan, can you come in here for a few?"

"Sure."

Sheridan was crazy about Lisette. Absolutely crazy about her. Sarah had a good point. Why wouldn't Lisette move to Houston and open a bookstore there? They could have a great life together. She had no doubt about that.

When she entered the office, the first thing Sheridan noticed was that the bookshelf was open.

"Have you been downstairs?"

"I have. Wait here. I'll be right back."

Sheridan sat on the couch wondering why she couldn't have gone downstairs with Lisette. It didn't really matter. Lisette would be back soon. Sheridan gave herself a pep talk about telling Lisette she was going back to Houston. And inviting Lisette to join her. She was a nervous wreck, which was a very unfamiliar emotion. Sheridan was used to being cool, calm, and controlled at all times. But what if Lisette said no? But why would she?

Lisette appeared at the top of the stairs wearing a black leather corset. Damn. Other thoughts flew from Sheridan's mind as she saw Lisette's milky white breasts on display. She needed Lisette. Right now. In every way she could have her.

Sheridan followed Lisette down the stairs into the secret room. Candles flickered from the desk, and she could make out something in the middle of the floor. She took her gaze off Lisette for a moment to realize it was a sleeping bag.

"It's as comfortable as I could make it," Lisette said.

"I'm not worried. Come here."

Sheridan kissed Lisette hard on her mouth while her hands peeled down the top of the corset and lovingly caressed her soft, firm, voluptuous breasts.

"Holy fuck," Sheridan whispered. "You are so fucking hot."

They continued to kiss as Lisette gently lowered them to the sleeping bag. It offered little protection from the dirt floor, but Sheridan didn't care. She had to have Lisette. She needed to take her and be taken by her.

"You're overdressed," Lisette said.

Sheridan struggled to get out of her clothes but soon lay naked under Lisette. She sucked and licked Lisette's nipples, amazed as always at how long they grew in her mouth. She ran her hands all over the leather corset, trying to figure out how to get to the rest of Lisette. She eventually found the zipper in the back and finally they lay skin to skin.

She brought her knee up to press it into Lisette's hot, wet center. Lisette moaned and began to rock against her, leaving a trail trickling down her thigh. Sheridan rolled on top of Lisette and, while suckling her breasts, found her center with her fingers.

In and out, she plunged her fingers, soon having four inside Lisette at once. Lisette arched her back, taking everything Sheridan could give her, and encouraging her onward. Lisette's head was thrashing back and forth on the ground which almost made Sheridan come on her own, but she fought the urge. The sight of Lisette so close to her release did things to her she'd never experienced before.

Lisette screamed out, sounds of pleasure echoing off the walls in their secret hidden room. Sheridan took deep breaths, still trying to hold off her impending orgasm. She finally withdrew her fingers and lay on her back, waiting impatiently for Lisette to come to her.

Lisette's world finally coalesced again. She slowly became aware Sheridan was no longer on top of her. She looked to her right and saw her lying naked there and desire coursed through her.

She climbed between Sheridan's legs and gazed at the wet, swollen beauty there. Sheridan was perfect, absolutely perfect and she was all hers. Lisette licked the length of Sheridan before darting her tongue deep inside her to taste her juices. She lapped at all of Sheridan's favorite spots. She felt Sheridan's hand on the back of her head and knew she was close.

Lisette licked and sucked her way back to Sheridan's clit. She focused all her attention on the tasty morsel, licking and sucking and licking some more. Sheridan finally cried out and Lisette continued, taking her over the edge one more time.

They lay together on the sleeping bag in the candlelit room for what seemed an eternity.

"Don't you have work to do?" Sheridan finally said.

"Probably. I'd rather stay here with you though."

"Mm. I get that. This was nice. Thank you."

"It was," said Lisette. "And it was my pleasure. We should use this room more often."

"It certainly gives us more privacy. That's for sure."

"Oui."

Lisette was feeling inordinate relief. She had been so concerned that morning. Something had felt off about Sheridan. About them. But she knew now it had all been in her imagination. She and Sheridan were fine. They would be fine. Forever. Or so she hoped.

"We should get dressed," Sheridan said.

"I suppose you're right. I'll keep the corset down here for future use. You seemed to really like it."

"That I did. You are so fucking hot anyway. But that corset? Damn. I can't even explain my visceral reaction."

"You demonstrated it quite well." Lisette laughed.

"That sleeping bag didn't provide much comfort." Sheridan got dressed. "These old bones can't lie on the ground that long."

"I know what you're saying. My back is a little sore. I'd ask for a back rub, but I think I know where that would end up."

"Yes." Sheridan laughed. "Right back on the floor."

In Lisette's office, they washed up and Lisette brushed her hair. "Do we look guilty?" she said.

"We look fine." Sheridan ran her hands through her hair. "Let's go see what's going on in the store."

"Where have you two been?" said Gabby.

"Down in the hidden room," Sheridan said. Lisette blushed and quickly turned away before anyone could notice.

"Cool. Did you find any answers?" Sarah said.

"None to help us, no," Lisette said.

"I want to go down there," said Gabby. "I want to look around. I feel like the answer to this mystery map is down there somewhere."

"Maybe tomorrow. Today is Louis's Day off and I need you up here."

"Okay. Tomorrow sounds good."

Lisette made a mental note to hide the candles and the sleeping bag.

"Oui. Tomorrow, we'll all go down there and scour every inch for clues."

The front door blew open and a group of tourists walked in. Lisette went over and greeted them and guided them back to the counter for coffee.

"It's very cold out there, no?" she said.

"Yes. That wind blows the rain right through you."

"What kind of books are you interested in?"

The tourists had heavy thick accents but did okay with English. Lisette finally directed them according to their book interests then came back to join her group.

"I'm famished," she said. "Sheridan? Will you take me to lunch?"

"Sarah and I ate before we got here. But I can have a coffee while you eat something."

They hurried up Rue Ste-Jean to a deli where Lisette ordered a sandwich and Sheridan ordered a café au lait.

"Does it ever not rain here?" Sheridan said.

"Oui. It was a very wet October for us. November seems to be much the same. We normally have crisp, sunny days in the autumn."

"Sunny days? I'll believe it when I see it." She laughed.

The rain had tapered off a bit by the time they walked back to the bookstore.

"This isn't as bad," said Sheridan.

"No. It's not horrible."

They found Sarah and Gabby at the back counter, perusing atlases.

"What if we're wrong?" said Gabby. "What if the map is in France or something? It may not even be here in Canada."

"I agree," said Sheridan. "It may be almost time to give up the ghost."

Lisette felt panic rise deep inside her.

"Are you serious? You don't mean that?"

"I don't know what I mean," said Sheridan. "I'm one who never gives up. But I feel like we've been on a wild goose chase."

"If you never give up, then don't now. Promise me? Promise me you won't give up?"

## CHAPTER SEVENTEEN

Lisette was reeling. Was Sheridan serious? Would she give up on the treasure hunt? Did that mean she'd give up on them? How could she? What about their future?

"I think we need to talk in my office," she said.

"Don't freak out," Sheridan said.

"Don't tell me what to do."

She let Sheridan in the office and locked the door behind them.

"What did you mean? You're really ready to quit searching?"

"I think I am," said Sheridan. "The X could be anywhere. We have no way of knowing it's even in Canada. And how long can I keep rescheduling my patients while searching for something we don't even know exists?"

"Your precious patients. What about me?"

"Come to Houston with me."

"Have you given this any thought? Or was it just some spur-of-the-moment decision?"

"Babe, you know I don't want to leave you," Sheridan said. "But I can't stay here indefinitely."

"So, you're going home and just thought I'd give up everything I've worked for and follow you?"

"You could open a bookstore in Houston. It's a big city. It needs more bookstores."

"But Quebec City is my home," said Lisette. "My family has been here for generations."

"I understand that."

"Do you?"

"Yes, but think of it as a new beginning."

"No," said Lisette. "I'm not walking away from everything important to me."

"I thought I was important to you."

"So did I."

"Lisette, please don't overreact."

"I'm not overreacting. The next thing you'll say is that I'm immature, just like she said all those years ago. Let me tell you something. I'm not immature. I've worked hard to get to where I am, and you won't belittle me into thinking otherwise."

"I'm not belittling you. We could do a long-distance relationship."

"You really have thought it all out, haven't you? Why was I not included in your decision-making?" Lisette was fuming.

"I haven't thought it all out. I'm trying to salvage us. If there even is an us. Which I thought there was, but maybe I'm wrong."

"Get out. Get out of my store and don't ever come back."

"I'll need to get my things from your house."

"Gabby can take you. Go. Now."

Lisette waited until she heard them leaving the store. Then, she wiped her eyes and went to cover the register. How dare Sheridan just announce in front of everyone that she no longer cared? About the treasure. About Lisette. About anything. The nerve of her.

And what kind of fool had she been? She had honestly allowed herself to dream of a future with Sheridan. Had Sheridan ever cared for her? She doubted it. She was just some fling to give her something to do while she was in Quebec City.

Well, Lisette Mouton was more than a fling. She was a woman who could give other women things Sheridan had barely gotten a taste of. She would have given Sheridan the world. If only she would have seen that.

Her phone buzzed. It was Sheridan.

*Let's not leave things like this.*

She tossed her phone on the counter. She wasn't about to reply. Sheridan who? That would be her new mantra as she rebuilt the wall around her heart that Sheridan had torn down.

However, now that she'd had a taste of a relationship, maybe it was time to get back to dating. She could find someone better than Sheridan. Someone who would truly care about her and her dreams. She wouldn't let Sheridan ruin her life. She'd use her as a stepping stone toward happiness and success.

Sheridan was in a foul mood as she packed her things and left Lisette's house, the house that had been her home for several weeks now. She'd miss it. She'd miss Lisette. She hadn't wanted things to end for them, but Lisette seemed to be insisting they do.

It was hard to believe they'd made passionate love in the hidden room mere hours earlier. Things had seemed so right. So real. How could Lisette just throw all that away? She tried to put herself in Lisette's shoes, but she couldn't. Lisette hadn't even given Sheridan a chance. She'd way overreacted and now they were over. Sure, Sheridan would move on, but she really didn't want to. One thing was certain. She'd never date again.

❖

Gabby drove Sarah and Sheridan to the airport.

"Can I ask what happened?" Gabby finally spoke.

"I wish I knew," Sheridan said. "I thought we'd discuss our future, but Lisette made it clear she didn't want a future with me."

"That sucks."

"Beyond."

Sarah and Sheridan were silent on the flight back to Houston. They landed at Bush Intercontinental and hired an Uber to take them to their respective homes. Sheridan felt claustrophobic in her large brick house. There was plenty of room, but the walls closed in on her. She'd never felt so alone in her life.

Sheridan was at the office at six thirty the next morning. Sarah arrived at seven.

"Weird being back, isn't it?" Sarah said.

"It is. But let's get to it. I want a full schedule today, Sarah. Have them move anyone they can to today, please."

"Yes, ma'am."

Sheridan lost herself in caring for her patients. She had new patients she had to run tests on to diagnose. She saw returning patients in for post-op appointments. And she saw patients who ended up being scheduled for surgery.

At three o'clock, she went into Sarah's office.

"Anything I need to know?" she said.

"Things are running smoothly."

"Great. Any messages for me?"

"No, ma'am. Nothing from Lisette either."

"I didn't ask about Lisette."

"You didn't have to."

Sheridan spun and left the room. She had more patients to see and that was what she lived for. Curing patients. Saving lives. Lisette would never, could never, comprehend that.

Lisette. Damn Sarah for making Sheridan think of her. She didn't need Lisette. She didn't need anyone. She was Dr. Sheridan Rousseau and that was all that mattered. And all that ever would.

Sheridan was exhausted when she got home around seven. She'd worked late seeing patients and then stayed after to make sure all her charting was done. Finally, she'd studied the cases of the patients she'd see the next day. It had been a long first day back, but she was back. And that's what mattered.

She poured herself two fingers of tequila and soaked in her Jacuzzi tub. She was tired and sore and knew this was just what she needed to get her prepared to sleep. But, when she got out of the tub, she wasn't sleepy, much to her chagrin.

Sheridan thought about doing some reading but decided against it. Books reminded her of Lisette, and she missed her something terrible. She sent her a text.

*Are you talking to me yet?*

She set her phone down, not really expecting a response. And she didn't get one. As long as she was thinking about Lisette, she pulled up her picture of the map on her phone. She stared at it, willing it to give her an answer. If she could figure out where the treasure was located, she would be able to see Lisette again. And maybe Lisette would love her again.

Love? Where the hell had that come from? Had they been in love? How deep had Sheridan's feelings been? She hated to admit it, but she truly had loved Lisette. And still did. And would do anything to win her back.

But...how had Lisette felt? That was a deeper question. And one to which Sheridan might never find an answer. Shit.

She climbed into bed and saw the clock turn twelve. Then one. She finally dozed and slept fitfully until her alarm went off at five. Shit. She was so damned tired. But she had patients who needed her, and she could get her beauty sleep another time.

Sheridan showered and dressed and drove to the office. She had another full day of office visits and would spend the following day in surgery. Life was good. Life was right. She was doing what she was meant to be doing. Lisette be damned.

"Good morning." Sarah placed a cup of coffee on Sheridan's desk.

"Good morning. How are you?"

"I'm good. Talked to Gabby this morning. Is it okay if I tell you that?"

"Of course. How's Gabby?"

"She's great. She's going to come visit for the new year."

"Right on. You two will have such a good time."

"I'm excited," said Sarah.

"You two make a cute couple. You should think about making it permanent."

Sarah laughed.

"We're too young to think like that. We're just having fun."

"Well, good. As long as it's still fun."

"It is."

Sarah went to her office, leaving Sheridan alone with her coffee and her thoughts. Why couldn't Lisette at least come for a visit? Just to see Sheridan and Houston. No strings attached.

But Sheridan knew she couldn't see Lisette no strings attached. She wanted strings. All the strings. She wanted to be tangled in strings with Lisette. She let out a heavy sigh just as her nurse told her her first patient had arrived.

It was another busy day for Sheridan and when she finally got home, all she wanted was to fall into bed. But her desire to get back to Lisette was greater. She opened her MacBook and began surfing the web, looking for maps of Quebec City and the surrounding area.

Maybe they'd been making it too difficult? Maybe the treasure had been right under their noses. But hours of studying maps left her in the same place she'd been when she left Quebec City. Tired and frustrated. And alone.

Sheridan scrubbed in for her first surgery of the day. It was a right anterior temporal lobectomy. Her patient had been suffering from epileptic seizures for years. He'd tried ablation surgery a year ago, but the seizures continued. Sheridan was positive this would resolve her patient's issue.

Four hours later, Sheridan removed her gown, washed up, and went out to see the man's wife. She'd known her as long as she'd known her patient and was happy to share the good news that the surgery appeared to get all of the lobe, and that the patient should be out of recovery in an hour or so.

The wife hugged Sheridan as tears of relief poured down her face. Sheridan hugged her back. This was why she did it. She helped people. She made their lives better, more livable. She had a meaning in life. Even if she had to be alone to live that life.

She headed back to surgery to scrub in for her next operation. This patient's disks had compressed and were pressing on nerves in her neck. Sheridan just had to put some titanium in between them to space them out and hold them in place. It was a relatively simple surgery. As she scrubbed, she wondered if she'd ever find someone who cared as much about her as her last patient's wife obviously cared about him. Did she want to? Probably not, if she was brutally honest. She didn't think she'd ever find anyone who understood how important her work was to her.

Lisette had pretended to understand, but when it came down to it, she hadn't. She'd expected Sheridan to drop her practice, and the patients who needed her. Sheridan couldn't do that. She wouldn't.

## CHAPTER EIGHTEEN

Lisette started her morning with a hot cup of coffee and a meeting with the Chamber of Commerce. The subject was Christmas decorations. Where would they be? Which businesses, if any, would be allowed to put up religious displays?

There were several heated arguments about the religious displays, but as it worked every year, they were allowed for anybody who wanted them. Quebec City still had a strong Catholic population who would have taken offense to only commercial decorations.

It didn't worry Lisette though. She'd decorate with snowmen and Santa and reindeer, but there would be a Nativity scene in front of the fireplace. She always did the best of both worlds to keep her regular customers happy. She didn't believe in the whole born in a manger thing, but she had many believers as patrons, and she didn't want to lose them.

She found Gabby at the back counter getting things ready for the day.

"Hey, boss. How was the meeting?"

"Fun and exciting. How are you today?"

"I'm great. Hey, have you heard from Sheridan?"

"No."

"That's really strange," said Gabby. "I'm surprised by that. Really surprised."

"If you must know, she's texted me twice. I've chosen not to answer."

"Why? What did her texts say?"

"It doesn't matter," said Lisette. "I'll never respond to her."

"Sounds like she might want to make things work? Surely, you're not opposed to that?"

"Quite frankly, I am. And now I'll be in my office, if you need me."

"Wait," said Gabby. "Why the chill? Toward me? What have I done besides be supportive?"

"You think I should entertain the thought of reconciling? After the way she treated me?"

"I watched the way she treated you for three weeks. She adored you. She would have done anything for you."

"Obviously, that's not true now." Lisette was trying to stay calm. She wanted to scream, shout, tear her bookstore apart. And she wanted to cry. Lord, how she wanted to cry. But she couldn't let anyone know how deep her feelings for Sheridan had run.

"It's bizarre. I can't believe she didn't even offer to take you with her. I really thought you'd eventually end up with her in Texas."

"As if I would leave this?" She motioned wildly at her surroundings. "This is my home. I'd never leave here to live in the United States. What kind of fool do you take me for?"

"Easy does it, boss. No need to get worked up. And especially not at me. I'm not Sheridan. I'm still here. But I won't be if you keep up the attitude with me."

"I'm sorry, Gabby. I guess I'm just emotionally raw right now. I'll hide in my office unless you need me for anything."

"Don't hide too long. That's not good for your mental health."

Lisette didn't respond. Gabby had no idea what was good for her mental health. Being alone was all she wanted or needed. She had work to do, wounds to lick, and life to contemplate. A life without Sheridan. How had she allowed herself to fall so completely for a woman in only three weeks?

How had she let her guard down? Or had she? Not really. Sheridan had wormed her way in through the cracks in the wall around her heart. Who could have possibly resisted her? Her charms? Her good looks? Her talents in bed?

Had it really only been a few days ago that Lisette had sat in this very chair with her legs over Sheridan's shoulders? It felt a lifetime ago. And everywhere Lisette went, she was reminded of Sheridan. Town Hall reminded her of Halloween. In her home, she still felt Sheridan's presence. And her office? How many times had they made love in there?

Maybe she needed to get away. Gabby and Louis could hold down the fort. Maybe she needed to go somewhere and search for the treasure. No. No treasure. That reminded her of Sheridan. She just needed to go on a brief vacation. But, where?

She loved Nova Scotia, but that had been ruined now. And she knew she could never go back to Banff National Park. And the States were out of the question. Where did that leave her?

She hadn't been to British Columbia since she was a young girl. Maybe it was time to pay it a visit. She searched for vacation spots on her computer and found the perfect spot. She reserved a place, made flight plans, and headed out to tell Gabby.

"I'm going away for a week," Lisette said. "Will you be able to handle things while I'm gone?"

"Where are you going?"

"Roberts Creek."

"Where's that?"

"The Sunshine Coast. I'm very excited. I'm leaving tomorrow."

"Good for you," said Gabby. "It'll really help to get away. I'm sure."

"I'm sure, too. I'll have my phone so you can text me if you have any questions or need anything at all."

Sheridan studied the maps again and again, wondering what she was missing. She had convinced herself the treasure had to be buried around Quebec City. She glanced at the clock. It was after two in the morning. She needed to get some sleep. Damn it. She knew she had to be getting close.

She climbed into bed and fell asleep hard. Her alarm went off at five thirty and she groaned as she turned it off. She needed more sleep. She needed to take better care of herself. But, why, really? Who cared if she took care of herself? No one. She had no one to care about her.

Not true, she had her patients. They cared that she took care of herself, so she was in optimum shape for treating them. She owed it to them to get a decent night's sleep. No maps tonight. Tonight, she'd sleep.

She got to her desk and pulled up the list of patients she'd be seeing that day. A couple of epileptic patients, a few neck patients, and she had a new patient. A middle-aged woman who had developed drop foot.

Sheridan was wide-awake with intrigue and excitement as she read over the woman's history.

"Morning, Dr. Rousseau." Sarah placed a coffee on her desk. "What are you reading?"

"Just getting up to speed on a new patient. How are you this morning?"

"Good. Tired, but good."

"I hear that. You won't believe what I was doing at two a.m."

"Texting Lisette?" Sarah said.

"No. Close though. I was looking at maps, trying to find the treasure."

"Still? I thought you'd let that go when we left Quebec City."

"I'm trying," said Sheridan. "But it calls to me. I feel like I'm so close and if I just keep staring at them, I'll see the answer."

"I think that's called being obsessive." Sarah laughed.

"Perhaps."

"Seriously, though. What are you going to do if you find where it could be? Fly back up?"

"That would be the plan."

"And leave your patients again?"

"It's not like I won't come back," Sheridan said.

"Something tells me if you see Lisette again, you'll never come back."

"You don't believe that."

"I do. Now, I'd better get to work before my boss gets ticked at me."

"Your boss is a bitch." Sheridan laughed.

"Royally."

The day went really well. Her post-op patients were doing very well. She scheduled a couple of other patients for surgery. Finally, it was four o'clock and it was time to meet with the woman with drop foot.

Sheridan walked into the room and there sat a stunning woman with shoulder length auburn hair and emerald eyes. She was tall and big-boned, but beautiful. Absolutely gorgeous. Sheridan realized she was staring. She walked over and shook the woman's hand.

"Dr. Rousseau," she said.

"I figured. I'm Madison Lombardi." Her voice was like warm honey.

"Tell me about your foot. When did this start?"

"It started a couple of months ago. I noticed every so often I couldn't raise my toes. Then I started dragging them and I knew I needed to be seen."

"Definitely." Sheridan wanted her to keep talking. She could have listened to her all day. "Was there any injury you sustained just before this happened?"

"No, ma'am."

"You don't have to call me ma'am. I looked at the MRI of your knee and hip and they seem normal, but I do see in your spine that we have a nerve root injury. Commonly referred to as a pinched nerve."

"So, it's not a stroke or anything?"

"No, ma'am. Your brain MRI looks perfectly normal."

"What a relief," Madison said. "So, will you prescribe physical therapy or something?"

"Actually, surgery is usually the first step. We want to catch it early, so it doesn't become permanent."

"Surgery? That seems extreme."

"Drop foot isn't something to mess around with," Sheridan said.

"Can I think about it?"

"Of course. But don't think too long. Time is of the essence."

"I understand."

"Might I suggest you schedule surgery just to get on the books and you can always cancel if you don't want to go through with it? We're scheduling about a month out at this point."

"That's a great idea," said Madison. "I'll do that."

"Great. I'll send in my assistant to make the appointment and give you some information on pinched nerves and drop foot. If you have any questions, don't hesitate to call us."

"Dr. Rousseau?"

"Yes?"

"Are you this kind and caring to all your patients?"

"I try to be, why?"

"I don't know. I just feel...like a connection with you," Madison said. She moved her head to the left and smiled up at Sheridan.

Sheridan's breath caught. She knew she was looking at Madison, but the tilt of her head, the way the light caught her, it was like Lisette was sitting there with her. She felt the shock of the image in every nerve in her body. Lisette. It was a gut punch. She coughed to cover her reaction.

"I'm glad you feel a connection. It's important to trust your surgeon."

"I think it's more than that and you know it."

Distracted by her emotions, and not really focusing on what Madison was saying, she had to replay the exchange in her mind. Surprised, she said, "Ms. Lombardi, are you flirting with me?"

"I'm certainly trying." Madison laughed.

"I'm flattered. I don't get involved with my patients, though."

"What a shame. Okay. I'll wait for your assistant."

Walking out of the exam room, Sheridan struggled to regain her composure. What had she done leaving Lisette in Quebec City? Madison Lombardi was everything she looked for in a woman. And she was here. In Houston. And it wouldn't take a wild goose chase to get together with her, but she wasn't Lisette. She'd never felt so connected to anyone the way she connected to Lisette, and she missed her.

She went into Sarah's office.

"Hey, Sarah. Patient in exam room five needs to schedule surgery for nerve root injury and she needs information sheets on drop foot."

"I'm on it."

"Thank you."

Sheridan reviewed the patients she'd see the next day. Sarah came by an hour later, purse on her shoulder.

"You're still here?"

"Mm. I guess I am."

"Why don't we grab a bite to eat? You can make yourself miserably full so all you'll want to do is go home and go to sleep."

Sheridan laughed.

"That's a great idea." She shut down her computer. "Let's go."

## CHAPTER NINETEEN

L isette's plane touched down in Vancouver's airport. As she flew in, she marveled at the different colored trees on display and knew in her heart she was doing the right thing for her. Looking out the window, she saw many trees had already lost their leaves, but some still had a few gold and red leaves hanging on.

She collected her luggage and picked up her rental to drive the forty-five minute trip to the ferry terminal. The ferry ride took only forty minutes and soon she was on the stunning Sunshine Coast. She drove to Roberts Creek and found her bed-and-breakfast. She unpacked and sat on the front porch watching people milling about the main streets.

Lisette's B and B was where the main streets met, an area known as Downtown. The area appeared to have shops, restaurants, and galleries. She couldn't wait to check it out. She was tired though. It had been an early flight. She went back inside to take a nap.

When she awoke, she was refreshed and hungry. She decided it was time to cruise the nearby area and find a late lunch or early dinner. She used her phone and found a restaurant that looked delicious and even purported to be LGBTQ friendly. She pulled on a light jacket and headed out.

The restaurant was quaint. It wasn't fancy which was good since she was wearing jeans and a sweater. She took a chance and sat outside.

"Good afternoon," the waitress said. "You're lucky to sit outside. We normally close the patio in November, but the weather has been very mild so far."

"I'm very lucky indeed."

"Have you been in Roberts Creek long?"

"I just got here. Took a nap and am about to go exploring."

"Excellent. You need food to explore. What can I get you?"

Lisette placed her order, and the waitress promised to be right back with her wine. Lisette enjoyed watching the people milling about. She carefully memorized many of the shops that were there and knew she'd have to be careful not to buy everything they sold in the cute artist's enclave.

As soon as she finished her meal, Lisette cut across the street to a bookstore. She meandered around, checking out the titles and comparing them to her own.

"Are you looking for anything in particular?" She turned to see a woman she guessed was in her fifties with short gray hair and piercing blue eyes.

"I actually own a bookstore, so I'm always curious what other bookstores sell."

"You own a bookstore? I thought I sensed a kindred spirit. Where are you from?"

"Quebec City."

"Oh, my," the owner said. "I was there once. I wouldn't want to own a bookstore there. Too much competition with the House of Treasures."

"Librarie De Trésors? You've been there? What a bizarre coincidence."

"Coincidence?

"I own it. That's my bookstore."

"Oh, my God. Are you serious? I found your bookstore and now you've found mine. It's kismet."

"Oui."

"I'm Jo, by the way."

"Lisette." She shook Jo's hand. It was warm and soft, and her handshake was firm. "What a pleasure to meet you."

"The pleasure is indeed mine. I have wanted to go back to your bookstore ever since I first set foot in it. It's my favorite. I've never felt more at home in a store in my life."

"Thank you. You're too kind."

"I'd love to swap war stories with you. That is, if you don't mind?"

"I'd love it," said Lisette.

"Would you join me for dinner?"

"I'd love to. Thank you."

"Great. Oh. I can't believe I met you. You're my shero."

"You are too kind," Lisette said again. "Though I'm glad to hear you enjoyed my little store."

"It's not little." The bell on the front door chimed. "I need to go help other customers. I'll see you back here at seven?"

"I'll be here." Lisette smiled. She was happy and relaxed and had a date for dinner. Life was looking up.

She wandered up and down the streets for a few hours, popping into stores and checking out their wares. She eventually made her way back to her B and B where she sat on the porch and searched in her phone for activities to do while she was there. She'd also ask Jo. Surely, she'd know of fun things to do there.

At six forty-five, Lisette changed into gray wool slacks and a black turtleneck sweater. There was a definite chill in the air now that the sun had set. The breeze from the water had picked up as well, so Lisette slipped her coat on and crossed the street to the bookstore.

Jo was sitting on the bench in front of her store when Lisette walked up. She stood when she approached.

"You look very nice," Jo said. "I'm afraid I'm still in my work clothes."

"You look great." Lisette wasn't lying. Jo had on black jeans and a blue chamois shirt that really made her eyes stand out.

"Come on," Jo said. "I'm parked around back. Let's take a little road trip."

"A road trip?" The thought that Lisette didn't know anything about Jo made her nerves tingle.

"Sure. Are you up for an adventure?"

"Always." She lied and tried to calm her nerves.

They climbed into Jo's 4Runner, and Jo headed out of town. They'd been driving about a half hour when Jo pulled down a dirt road. The conversation between them had been easy but they were both silent now as Jo focused on the dark road ahead of her.

They hadn't gone much further when she pulled in front of what appeared to be a cabin.

"We're here," said Jo.

"Where's here?"

"Just you wait and see."

They entered the cabin. Hanging on one wall was a large rainbow flag as well as other flags Lisette didn't recognize.

"I hope you're hungry," Jo said.

"Starving."

"Do you eat meat? I guess I should have asked that. Although they serve a mean salmon as well. If you eat fish?"

Lisette laughed.

"I eat meat. And I love seafood. It's nice to know I have options."

The restaurant was half full and Jo and Lisette were seated by the travertine fireplace.

"Not a bad location," Jo said.

"Not at all. This place is amazing."

"It's a little-known secret around here. You have to know it's here. And getting here is a trek. But it's well worth it."

"I can't wait to find out," said Lisette.

Sheridan missed Lisette. There was no getting around it. She missed her as a person but also missed the companionship. Maybe her time in Canada had been meant to open her eyes to what was missing in her life. Why couldn't she find companionship here? Why shouldn't she?

That Friday night, after a day full of surgeries, Sheridan showered, dressed in black slacks and a purple shirt, and headed to her favorite watering hole. It wasn't a gay bar, per se, but professional lesbians had taken it over and made it their own on Friday and Saturday nights.

Sheridan sat at the bar, nursing her Don Julio when the bartender put another glass in front of her.

"Where did this come from?" Sheridan said.

"The woman at the other end of the bar."

Sheridan glanced down to the end and saw Madison Lombardi sitting there. Sheridan raised her glass in a toast and Madison picked up her purse and walked over.

"May I sit with you?" she said.

"Of course. And thank you for the drink."

"My pleasure. Anything for the woman who's going to save my life."

"I'm not saving your life." Sheridan laughed. "I'm making it much better though."

"Mm. I'll drink to that."

"What brings you here on a Friday night?" Sheridan said.

"You know, just unwinding."

"What do you do? I mean, for a living?"

"I'm a curator at the Health and Science Museum."

"Impressive," said Sheridan.

"I don't know about that. It pays the bills. And I enjoy it."

"I've always enjoyed our museums."

"Well, you're welcome, then."

"Thank you for the drink, also."

"Again," said Madison. "You're welcome. And you're not a cheap date."

Sheridan laughed.

"I have expensive taste. What can I say?"

"Can't argue with that. You earn it. Might as well spend it."

"Exactly. Can I return the favor? What are you drinking?"

"I want to try what you're having."

"Do you like tequila?" Sheridan said.

"I don't dislike it. I've never just sipped it though."

"You're in for a treat then."

Sheridan ordered Madison two fingers of Don Julio. She watched as Madison took a hesitant sip.

"Oh, wow," said Madison. "This is delicious."

"Right?"

"So, tell me, what other expensive tastes do you have?"

"I'm not about to disclose all my secrets to a patient."

"Can't we pretend, just for a night, that I'm not your patient?"

"No can do. Not for a night. But maybe for a dinner?"

"Hm. That's quite a compromise," Madison said.

"That's my offer. Take it or leave it."

"I'll take what I can get, I guess. Where shall we have dinner?"

"I'm buying so you get to choose."

"That's not very butch. You need to take charge."

Sheridan was starting to get annoyed with Madison. Did she really want to spend a couple of hours at dinner with her? She supposed it was better than spending time alone. She did enough of that.

"Fine," she said. "Finish your drink. We'll Uber to a restaurant I like."

"I'm sure there are restaurants within walking distance."

"You had your chance to choose. You left it to me. We're going to one of my favorites."

"Oh, my. Now you're sounding like a true butch. Be still my foolish heart."

Sheridan pulled out her phone and ordered an Uber. She finished her drink and sat waiting for Madison to be ready. She glanced at her phone.

"Uber's almost here. Finish your drink."

Madison downed the sip of tequila that was left, got off her barstool, and took Sheridan's hand.

"What's this?" Sheridan lifted up their interlocked fingers.

"Just making sure you don't change your mind."

Madison snuggled up against Sheridan in the back seat. Sheridan was decidedly uncomfortable. Madison had made it quite clear she was interested. Sheridan had tried to make it crystal clear she wasn't. She hoped the night ended on a friendly note.

The Uber dropped them off at one of Houston's upscale steakhouses. It was far and away Sheridan's favorite restaurant. She just hoped Madison wouldn't sour that for her.

"I've never been here," Madison said. "It's supposed to be fantastic."

"That it is. Trust me."

"Oh, I do."

They split a bottle of wine while they waited for their meals.

"Are you from Houston originally?" Sheridan was determined to keep them on safe ground.

"You can't tell from my accent? I was raised in Dallas."

"Ah."

"And you?"

"Born and raised," said Sheridan.

"And destined to die here?"

Sheridan paused before answering. She'd always thought she was destined to die here, but now she wasn't so sure. Visions of Quebec City danced in her head. Would she ever get back there? Much less, get back with Lisette? Would she be willing to give up her practice in Houston to practice in a foreign country?

"That's a great question," she finally said.

"Where else? I mean, Houston is an amazing city. Where else would you consider being?"

"You just never know," said Sheridan. "You never know."

## CHAPTER TWENTY

Lisette was up early the next morning. She'd thoroughly enjoyed her evening with Jo but was ready to explore on her own. Jo had given her some suggestions of things to do and even offered to close her shop to show Lisette around.

Lisette liked Jo. And at least she lived in the same country. But Lisette wasn't looking for romance. As a matter of fact, she was trying to forget about romance. She didn't need love and passion in her life. Her store had been enough for her for years and would be enough for years to come.

She leisurely made her way down Roberts Creek Road to Beach Avenue. It was cold but promised to warm up to sixteen degrees later. She'd dressed in layers accordingly. She pulled her coat closed and zipped it up to brace against the cool breeze coming off the water.

Her adventures began with a kayak tour of the local area. The water was cold, but soon her butt was numb so she could no longer complain. She paddled at her own pace most of the time, occasionally having to paddle a little faster to catch up to the group again.

Lisette thoroughly enjoyed the lush green of the mountains contrasted with the blue of the water. She couldn't remember a time when she'd felt as relaxed as she did there. She saw deer nibbling on something at one point and, at another, heard someone shouting and looked up to see a pod of dolphins frolicking in the waves. It wasn't graceful, but she managed to get out of the kayak after a few hours and, once she got her land legs back, she followed the street to a lovely café.

She couldn't get enough of the hot coffee to defrost after hours on the water. She had finally warmed up enough to order granola with vanilla yogurt and banana. It was delicious and so very different from her normal breakfast choices. She felt like she was in another world.

"I'm feeling like I'm ready to continue my explorations," Lisette told her waitress. "Where do you recommend I go next?"

"Have you seen the mandala?"

"I have not. But I've heard about it. Should I check it out?"

"I'd highly recommend it. And you're not far. Would you like a coffee to go?"

Lisette graciously declined another cup of coffee. It was strong, much like its surroundings, but she was already afraid she'd be floating the rest of the day. She paid her bill, pulled her coat on, and set off to find the famous Roberts Creek Mandala.

There were several tourists admiring the mandala when she arrived. And once she got closer, she could see why. The mandala was obviously dedicated to music and had a lovely robin at its center.

Lisette read up on the tradition of the mandala that began when a group of people got together to paint over graffiti in the parking area. That was in 1997 and the tradition was still going strong, with a different theme every year.

While Lisette had heard of mandalas and had seen one or two, nothing prepared her for the outright beauty of where she stood. Community members contributed under one man's supervision until it was complete. Then, a select few dancers danced on the mandala to signify its completion.

"Gorgeous, isn't it?"

Lisette glanced up to see a woman who looked to be a few years older than herself watching her.

"It truly is. Breathtaking, really."

"You're not from around here, are you?" said a woman standing next to the first.

"No. Are you?"

"No, but this is a very special place for us."

"I can understand that. This place is amazing," said Lisette.

"We're being rude," said the first woman. "Allow me to introduce us. I'm Helen and this is Darlene."

"It's a pleasure to meet you two. My name is Lisette."

"That name, that accent," said Darlene. "Where are you from?"

"I'm from Quebec City, born and raised."

"That's someplace we've always wanted to visit," said Helen.

"You definitely should. It's beautiful there."

"Would you give us a private tour?" Helen said. Something about the way she said it made Lisette uncomfortable.

"I'd be happy to show you around," she said.

"What brings you to Roberts Creek Mandala?" Darlene said.

"I'm just here on vacation and looking for things to do. What brings you here?"

"We're celebrating. We met here fifteen years ago today."

"You met here?"

"We did. Both of us on vacation. Separately, of course. We ran into each other here and the rest, as they say, is history," said Helen.

"Is that right?"

"We got married a year later. We're here celebrating our fifteenth anniversary of meeting, though."

"That's amazing." Lisette meant it. She was happy for these strangers for finding something that she was certain would elude her for the rest of her life.

"Thank you," said Darlene.

Lisette turned to Helen.

"Where do you two live?"

"We settled on California. Dar lived in Texas, and I lived in Missouri, but we wanted to live somewhere we felt safer, so we bought a house in Napa Valley."

Lisette thought that must have cost a pretty penny. She'd heard of Napa Valley and had seen pictures. It was beautiful. Not as beautiful as her home, of course, but beautiful in its own way.

"That's great. I'm glad you did that. It's important to feel safe."

"Do you feel safe in Quebec City?"

"Always."

"Good. As you said, that's important. So how is it we find you at the mandala this afternoon?"

"I'm on vacation. I'm staying nearby, and this was recommended by several people. I'm glad I came."

"I'm glad you came, too," Helen said.

Lisette looked at her new friends. She guessed they were in their early fifties. Darlene had short silver hair slicked back, and Helen had dishwater blond hair. They made a handsome couple.

"Have you ever been with a woman?"

Lisette was taken aback but decided to answer honestly.

"Yes. I'm a lesbian."

"Have you ever been with two women?" Darlene said.

"Excuse me?"

"We're staying not far from you. We could have some fun," Helen said.

"Thank you," Lisette said. "I'm flattered. But truth be told, I'm nursing a broken heart so I'm not really looking for anything right now."

"No strings attached," Darlene said.

"Thank you. But, no. I think I need to go warm up now. It was nice meeting you two."

Fighting the urge to run away as fast as she could, Lisette took measured steps until she had gotten herself good and lost, but even lost she felt safer than she had with Darlene and Helen.

Saturday morning, Sheridan slept until seven and was somewhat groggy when she finally woke up. She'd had too much to drink the previous night, but not enough to make her lose her resolve about doctor-patient relationships.

Madison was indeed a very attractive woman, but she was Sheridan's patient first and foremost. And, although Sheridan had been contemplating leaving the practice, she wanted to do it on her terms and not because she got kicked out. And she really had no reason to leave. She just couldn't let go of the fantasy that she and Lisette would get back together. Then she would join a practice in Quebec City.

It was a lovely daydream, but reality was that she was in Houston and Lisette was in Canada and hadn't responded to any of Sheridan's attempts to connect. Although, what it would hurt to at least keep in touch, Sheridan didn't know.

So, there she was, all alone on a warm Saturday morning with nothing to do and no one to do it with. Depression threatened to intrude on her day. She wouldn't, couldn't let that happen. She'd battled it all her life and had sunk to low levels of despair in the past. She wouldn't do that this time. The climb out was often treacherous, and she didn't want to expend her energy on that again.

Her coffee maker beeped, letting her know the magical elixir was ready. She poured herself a cup and took it out to her deck. Her backyard was in better shape than it should have been. She had a crew that took care of it for her, which was nice. They kept her lawn mowed and the bushes trimmed. At the moment, she wished she didn't have them because a day of yardwork would have suited her just fine.

She needed to find something productive to do before she lost her mind. She took her coffee back inside and sat at her desk. She opened her MacBook and started studying maps of Quebec City. She sincerely believed she was missing something, believed if she just looked at things a little differently, she'd find the treasure.

But the map didn't seem to represent anything in Quebec City. Not the Plains of Abraham, not the Notre Dame Basilica, not even the Fairmont Chateau Frontenac. Nothing had the right outline. She got another cup of coffee and returned to her map.

While Sheridan truly believed the treasure had to be in Quebec City, looking at all the sights was depressing her. She really missed the walled city. Not as much as she missed Lisette, of course. But the city had a certain charm to it and Sheridan hoped she'd get to experience it again.

She closed her MacBook and stared into space while she finished her second cup. Her mind wouldn't slow down. She almost opened the computer again, but made herself step away. She put her empty cup in the dishwasher and went down the hall to take a shower.

Clean and dressed in cargo shorts and a T-shirt, Sheridan got in her Tacoma and headed to the Montrose District. The district had been the gayborhood for decades. Now it was still a place for misfits, but they weren't just gays and lesbians. It was still an eclectic neighborhood, and she thought it would be nice to find a place to simply people watch.

She pulled into the parking lot of the Human Bean. A chai latte was calling her, and she could sit at the window and watch the car and foot traffic on Pressler Street. Neither of the traffics disappointed. She saw everything from Rivians to Teslas to old beaters with rainbow stickers.

The people who walked by varied in appearance as well. There were young families and groups of young adults with hairstyles that had Sheridan wondering if she'd ever been that young and dumb. Middle-aged people passed by with tattoos and piercings that rivaled their younger counterparts.

"Dr. Rousseau?"

Sheridan looked up to see Sarah standing with a cup of coffee and a Danish.

"Have a seat, Sarah. What are you up to this morning?"

"I'm meeting some friends at the park. We're going to hang out and play Frisbee and listen to music."

"Do you have time to sit for a minute?"

"Of course." Sarah sat across from Sheridan. "Would you like some of my Danish?"

"No, thanks." Her stomach chose that moment to growl angrily. "Maybe I'll go get one of my own. Hang tight. I'll be right back."

"So, what are you doing this weekend?" Sarah said when Sheridan returned.

"I have no idea. I'm bored and restless."

"Not a good combination."

"Well, we had a pretty busy few weeks. I guess this is just the letdown."

"Maybe. Have you looked at any maps?"

"Have you?" Sheridan said.

"I asked you first."

"I've done little else. If I'm not at work, I'm scouring maps, trying to see where the treasure is."

Sarah laughed.

"I hate to admit it, but same here."

"Any luck?"

"None. I've pretty much ruled out the western third of the country."

"I've been focusing on Quebec City. I have a feeling the treasure was literally right under our noses."

"Maybe. I don't know. And I guess we'll never know now, will we?"

"I hate admitting defeat."

"Sometimes we just have to accept that things didn't work out."

"Maybe," Sheridan said. "I don't know. I still can't believe Lisette won't even text me back. It's like I did something horrible besides returning to help my patients."

"It is puzzling. I thought you two were somehow going to go the distance. I couldn't figure out how, but I thought the two of you would, so I didn't worry about it."

"Well, maybe if I find the treasure she'll speak to me again."

"I hope so. For your sake." Sarah took the last bite of her Danish. "That was good. Not as good as what we got in that little bakery on Rue Ste-Jean, but good for Houston."

"Talk about a dichotomy. Quebec City and Houston. Worlds apart and not just geographically."

"Right? And where does your heart lie? Or do I need to ask?"

"I ask myself that daily, Sarah. Every single day."

## CHAPTER TWENTY-ONE

Sheridan left the coffee shop shortly after Sarah left to meet her friends. Maybe she needed friends. She was sure she had some, though. The other doctors in her practice for starters. Were they truly friends? Or were they merely acquaintances who she worked with?

Deciding they were definitely the latter, Sheridan headed home and picked up her golf clubs. An afternoon on the links would surely cure what ailed her. She drove to the country club and was soon on the course proving that she definitely needed more lessons.

She finished just after six o'clock and was anything but proud of her score. She went to the clubhouse to order a burger and a beer. She'd earned both.

"Looked like you weren't having your best day," the bartender said.

"I definitely was not. But it was still fun."

"Good. I'll buy your first beer as a consolation prize."

Sheridan laughed.

"Much appreciated." She sat on a barstool and watched the attractive bartender wait on other golfers. The bartender had black hair that fell halfway down her back and light eyes the color of the sky. Sheridan figured the bartender was almost as tall as she was and even skinnier. She was easy on the eyes and Sheridan was conscious of actually relaxing for the first time in a while.

"My name's Lisa. And you might you be?" The bartender's eyes bored into Sheridan as if searching for the answer to a mystery.

"I'm Sheridan. Nice to meet you."

"Your burger won't be up for a while. As you can see, this place is a zoo today. Can I get you another beer?"

"Please."

"I don't think I've seen you before. And I'm sure I would have remembered you." Lisa winked.

"I usually golf at Hermann. Although, I don't even golf there nearly enough."

"I'd offer to help you, but I wouldn't even know which end of the golf club to hold."

"I could teach you." The words were out of Sheridan's mouth before she could stop them. "I mean, if you're interested."

"I do appreciate that. Really, I do. But golf just doesn't interest me."

"You're just here for the beer, huh?"

"Pretty much." Lisa laughed.

Sheridan felt a sharp pain in her chest, noting the sound of Lisa's laugh was very close to Lisette's.

She enjoyed watching Lisa cruise behind the bar, taking orders and serving drinks. She enjoyed the way Lisa's tight shorts clung to her adorable ass, but Lisa wasn't Lisette and never could be. She realized she was pushing herself into thinking about a mindless physical encounter. It felt like a betrayal of Lisette.

"Can I get another one, Lisette?" Sheridan said. Lisa turned and stared at her.

"Lisette? Cute, but it's Lisa."

"Oh, my God. I'm so sorry. I know that." Sheridan couldn't believe she'd called Lisa the wrong name. Clearly, she had some work to do. "I tell you what. Donate my burger to the cause. I'm out of here."

"Are you sure? It's not a big deal. I mean, at least it was close."

"No, thank you. I need to go."

At home, Sheridan slipped into board shorts and a T-shirt and climbed into the hot tub on her deck. The bubbles felt good against her sore muscles. Her shoulders ached from the hours on the golf course.

She closed her eyes and let her mind wander back to Quebec City. She would have given anything to have Lisette sitting there with her. They could make out like teenagers then go inside and make love together. *Shit*. She needed to do something. She needed to make decisions, difficult though they might be.

It would take a lot to leave her practice in Houston. It would involve notifying the other doctors and her patients, obviously, but then she'd have to pass the MCCOE, the Canadian Medical Qualifying exam. Next she would have to complete certifying exams with the Royal College of Physicians, no easy task. If she completed those steps, she'd have to apply for a Provincial License and demonstrate a proficiency in French. Not to mention all the steps involved in immigration. It was so much to consider. If she moved forward with this, would Lisette even be willing to consider taking her back? Would she even have a chance? Was she thinking about destroying her career and reputation on a whim? Would it be worth it? She didn't know, but the idea wouldn't leave her mind. It was all she could think about. And she needed to decide.

What about Lisette? Would she welcome Sheridan back? Or would she tell her to stay away? She wanted to believe she'd take her back. Sheridan hadn't called Lisette immature. That was something Lisette imagined based on a previous partner. Wait. Partner? Was that what Lisette had been? Or had she been Sheridan's girlfriend? They'd only been together a matter of weeks. So, she supposed they'd been dating. Was that really it? Dating? She needed, craved so much more from Lisette. Would Lisette ever reciprocate?

She dried her hands and sent Lisette a text.

*Thinking about coming back. Would I be able to see you?*

Setting the phone back on the table, she leaned her head back and closed her eyes again. All she could do now was wait. Waiting was definitely not her forte, but it was up to Lisette now to determine Sheridan's next move.

❖

Lisette fell more in love with Roberts Creek every day she spent there. It was Sunday and Jo had taken the day off to spend with her. They drove to Cliff Gilker Park to start the day with a couple of hours to hike and check out the gorgeous waterfalls.

They started off on the Yellow Trail and followed it downhill.

"What's the name of this creek again?" Lisette paused and looked at the creek flowing just under the slats.

"Clack Creek."

"It's really rolling."

"Yes, so take care not to slip. I'd hate to lose you."

Lisette laughed.

"Didn't you say something about a waterfall?"

"I may have mentioned at one indeed. And you'll see it as we take this turn up ahead."

Lisette froze at the sight. She took her phone out and snapped picture after picture of the high powerful falls. Lisette couldn't tear her focus away from the water as it tumbled over the rocks.

"Yoo-hoo! Earth to Lisette," Jo called.

"Hm?" Lisette finally responded.

"How about a selfie?"

"Yes. We need one."

They stood together and took turns taking pictures. Lisette was absolutely loving the show that nature was putting on for them. She wanted to stay there all day.

"Come on," said Jo. "There are more views from different trails."

"If you insist."

The rest of the two hours did not disappoint. Though, it did occur to Lisette that Jo seemed more than a little determined to woo Lisette, and Lisette was most decidedly not available for wooing. She let Jo know on multiple occasions she was recovering from a broken heart and not interested in pursuing anything with Jo, regardless of how kind and flattering she was.

Jo took Lisette up the coast to a taproom for lunch. They sat upstairs and Lisette listened attentively to all the beer options recommended for each item on the menu. She finally decided on a beer and burger combo and she and Jo relaxed and discussed how beautiful the hike had been that morning.

"I really want to thank you for taking the day off to show me around," said Lisette.

"We have another stop after this, so don't fill up too much."

"I couldn't eat another bite."

"No, but perhaps you could drink something? And that's all I'll say."

"Hm. I'm curious. But I won't ask any questions since you obviously want to surprise me."

"Thank you. Now, what have you enjoyed most about being in Roberts Creek?"

"I love the water," Lisette said.

"Too bad you live so far from it."

"Well, we have the Saint-Charles river. And of course, the St. Lawrence river which separates us from Lévis. So, we have beaches and water. But no ocean. And we do have our waterfalls, of course."

"If you moved here, you'd be by the ocean all the time."

"And I wouldn't be in my home. Or the home of generations before me. No. I love to visit, but Quebec City is my home."

"I love the look on your face when you talk about your home. You truly love it there," said Jo.

"Oui. I do indeed."

After lunch, they drove to the center of Gibsons to a cidery so Lisette could do some cider tasting. Lisette was thoroughly enjoying herself, but she was getting worn down from deflecting Jo's constant advances.

After Lisette had had a few samples of cider, Jo, who was drinking coffee, asked the questions Lisette knew she had been wanting to ask since they'd met.

"What really brought you to Roberts Creek? It's a long way to come with no plans and no agenda."

"I have no agenda. I just needed to get away for a few days."

"Why?"

"If you must know, I just got out of a relationship. It ended badly and I needed to get out of my head and away from memories for a while."

"I'm sorry." Jo placed her hand over Lisette's. Lisette pulled her hand away.

"It's okay," she said. "I'm enjoying my time out west. And I appreciate your taking the time to show me around. But please understand. I'm not even remotely in the market for anything."

"Fair enough. Can't blame a girl for trying though."

"I appreciate that." Lisette had maxed out on Jo time. "Let's head back now. I want to have some alone time in my B and B."

"Of course."

Lisette was relieved when Jo finally pulled up in front of her cottage.

"May I take you to dinner tonight?" Jo said. "No strings attached, of course."

"Thank you. But I think I'd like to be alone the rest of the day. I'll stop by the bookstore to see you tomorrow."

"I look forward to it."

Lisette went into her cottage, closed the door behind her, and hung her heavy jacket on the coat rack. Roberts Creek and the neighboring areas were truly breathtaking. She was grateful to Jo for showing her around. But she wasn't interested in pursuing a relationship with Jo. Once she was back in Quebec City, she was certain Jo would never cross her mind. If only she could get Jo to realize that without being rude or hurtful.

She bundled back up again an hour later and went in search of a light dinner. She found a café and had a delicious panini and another glass of cider. The café served cider from the cidery she'd been visiting earlier, which made her very happy.

Back at her cottage, Lisette turned on the gas fireplace and took a book from the bookshelf to read. She let herself relax, completely relax, for the first time since Sheridan left.

The book was too good to put down and it was early Monday morning when she climbed into bed. She was up at eight and decided to go for a walk around the area before the crowds gathered. It was a cool, crisp morning and she could see her breath as she paused to look in store windows and greet shopkeepers preparing for the day.

She noticed an open coffee shop so went back to the cottage to get her book then went to the shop for much needed caffeine and a croissant. The coffee was strong, so it tasted great and woke her up.

The croissant left much to be desired. She didn't finish it. Instead, she decided to find a real restaurant and get some breakfast.

Lisette followed her nose and found a charming place to eat. She devoured her breakfast and lost count of how many cups of coffee she'd had. With a full belly, she took out her phone and googled things to do in Roberts Creek. As much as she'd love to curl up in her cottage and read, she didn't want to waste a day in this cute area of the country.

She went to the cottage and changed into some jeans and a green cable-knit sweater. She drove to Sechelt to check out the Indigenous history. She found the shíshálh Nation tems swiya Museum. She spent a couple of hours there and thoroughly enjoyed herself. She learned a lot about the native people of the area.

Lisette was getting used to doing things by herself again. Did she miss Sheridan? Of course. Did she miss the things they did together? Definitely. But was she okay on her own? Without a doubt.

She spent the next couple of hours at the pub on the water, where she enjoyed several local ciders and delicious fish and chips. She topped off lunch with a gooey chocolate caramel cake. The food was wonderful and the location with the seaplanes flying in and out kept her entertained.

She drove back to Roberts Creek and took a nap before dinner. She decided on a light fare for dinner. She drank cider, visited with other customers and the wait staff, and really enjoyed herself. Two hours later, she was back in her cottage, in front of the fire, finishing her book.

## CHAPTER TWENTY-TWO

S unday morning found Sheridan in front of her MacBook, looking up maps of Quebec City from around the time of the French revolution. She wouldn't give up. She couldn't. She needed to solve the mystery, get back to Quebec City, and make a life with Lisette.

The only way Lisette would let her anywhere near her was if she knew where the treasure was. Sheridan truly believed this. So, she studied maps until she was cross-eyed. She had been scouring the websites for three hours and was nowhere near closer to her goal. She gave up. For the moment. Certainly not for good.

She thought about going out again, but being around people didn't appeal to her. She grabbed her phone off the desk and flipped through social media, but soon lost interest. She was just about to close out when she saw a notice on a friend's page. Her friend had finished fifty lessons in Duolingo.

Sheridan thought she should try that. The only language she spoke was English with a little Latin thrown in for medical purposes. How impressed would Lisette be if Sheridan could converse with her in her native tongue? Besides, if she did make this change in her life, French was a necessary component.

She signed up for Duolingo and began French lessons. They weren't hard, though even she could tell her accent left much to be desired. Luckily, the app couldn't laugh at her. She spent the next few hours learning basic words and phrases. She got frustrated at some things. For instance, there were at least three ways to say "in." What was up with that?

At four o'clock, she realized she hadn't eaten all day. She checked the fridge, but there was nothing in there but a few beers and some butter. She ordered a pizza online and went back to the maps.

As she ate dinner, Sheridan expanded her search area. She looked at maps of Beauport, Saint-Roch, Gatineau, and finally Lévis. There was so much geography to cover, and she still didn't know if she was even close to being on the right path.

Beauport seemed promising. It was east of downtown Quebec City and had a beach. As Sheridan dug deeper though, logic won out. Anything buried on the beach centuries ago would be long gone by now.

It was getting late when she began studying Lévis. Soon, she could barely keep her eyes open, so she closed the MacBook and climbed into bed. She needed a good night's sleep before seeing patients the next day.

❖

"How was your weekend, Dr. Rousseau?" Sarah said.

Sheridan sighed heavily.

"I attempted to golf Saturday. But Sunday was spend studying maps. I feel like I'm getting closer, though. I really think I'm almost there."

"That would be wonderful. I do hope you solve the mystery soon because I know you and you won't rest until you've found it."

"This is very true. I fear it's become an unhealthy obsession, but I suppose there are worse obsessions to have." Sheridan laughed.

"True. At least there's a treasure at the end of this."

"There'd better be anyway."

"Right? We don't even know what we're looking for," said Sarah. "But if you want an assistant to go back to Quebec City with you, you know where to find me."

"That I do."

Maps and treasures were the furthest thing from Sheridan's mind as she saw patients. She listened, really listened, to everything they said and even what they didn't say. Each patient was a puzzle and Sheridan prided herself on solving puzzles.

She left the office at seven, stopped for a quick dinner, went home, and climbed in the hot tub. She was tense from the day's work and the previous day spent bent over her MacBook. The hot tub felt amazing.

But as she sat there, her brain slowly quit replaying the issues her patients were having and began to tease her about not having been able to solve the mysterious map problem. She sat in the tub, eyes closed, and watched the slideshow in her brain. She revisited every map she'd ever looked at and wondered why she hadn't found the buried treasure.

She dried off, put on some pajama pants and an T-shirt, and powered up her MacBook. She was close. She knew it. She could feel it. And she vowed not to quit until she found the hiding spot.

Where was she? Oh, yes. Lévis. It was right across the St. Lawrence from Quebec City, so would make a logical place to hide the treasure. She stared at the pictures of the map in her phone and willed herself to see the outline in Lévis. She soon grew too tired to focus so turned off the laptop and went to bed.

Lévis stayed with her throughout the next day at work and as soon as she could get away, she raced home to study it some more. She found a church that had been there since before the Revolution. It had a graveyard attached to it. She was wide-awake as she studied the layout.

It definitely seemed to match the map. Everything lined up perfectly. The X would be somewhere in the graveyard. Was that right? Or was she imagining things because she wanted this so badly?

No. It was true. The treasure could easily be buried in a grave. Or by itself in a graveyard. It was genius.

Sheridan was beyond excited. She texted Lisette, Sarah, and Gabby.

*I'm sure I found it. When should we come back?*

She stared at her phone, willing Lisette to answer. Sarah did immediately.

*I'm ready when you are.*

Next came Gabby.

*Where? Are you sure? God, I hope you're right.*

Nothing from Lisette. Sheridan sent her an individual text.

*Let's put our differences aside and try again. Please? Let's find the treasure.*

An hour later, when she still hadn't heard from Lisette, Sheridan went to bed. Feeling more dejected than elated at that point.

Lisette sat on her bed staring at Sheridan's messages. Had she really found the location of the secret treasure? Lisette's heart raced. How amazing would that be? Would Sheridan share the location with her without coming back up? Not likely. Not that Lisette could blame her.

She replayed the last few moments they'd spent together, just as she had a million times before. Sheridan had been like the others before her who thought Lisette's bookstore was more of a hobby than the fulfillment of a lifelong dream. Although she hadn't come right out and said it, she had actually thought Lisette would abandon her dream as well as her home, to go to the States. The nerve.

Lisette felt her pulse racing and knew she needed to calm down. She had a decision to make. And she needed to make it with a clear head. She put her phone down and lay back in her bed. Sleep did not come easy for her and when it did, it was filled with unwelcome erotic dreams of Sheridan.

"Did you see Sheridan's text last night?" Gabby said when Lisette arrived in the morning.

"I did."

"Did you reply?"

"I did not. If she can figure out the location, then so can we."

"You know," Gabby said, "she could just go to the location and claim the treasure and we would never know. I think you should invite her back."

"To what end? We get the treasure. *Maybe*. But what happens then?"

"We split it four ways and go about our lives."

"I don't know if I can see Sheridan again and simply go on with my life."

"Have you talked to her at all since she's been gone?"

"I have not," said Lisette.

"She was really into you. And you were into her. I don't know what was said the day they left, but I don't think you can blame her for getting back to her practice. She is a doctor, for fuck's sake."

"She had a lot of nerve. She thought I would drop everything and move to Houston."

"So, she asked you to go with her?" Gabby seemed shocked. "And that pissed you off?"

"Women don't seem to understand what this bookstore means to me. Let alone that Quebec City is in my blood."

"I know Sheridan gets it. All of it. But she wanted you with her. That has to count for something."

"No. It showed complete disregard for my life. My dreams."

"Whatever. I think you overreacted."

"And what you think is inconsequential."

"Why didn't you attempt a long-distance relationship?"

"I don't need anyone that badly," Lisette said. "I've been fine on my own for years and will continue to be."

"If only you could have seen you when you were with her."

"Enough."

"Text her back," said Gabby. "Set some ground rules if you have to. But you need to at least acknowledge that she may have found the treasure location."

"I'll think about it."

Lisette thought of little else. It was very difficult to concentrate on balancing the books that morning. She stayed in her office, alone, for hours while she debated the best course of action. Every ounce of her being longed to have Sheridan come back, if only for a few days.

What she wouldn't give to have those strong arms around her again. She checked her watch. It was one thirty. What time would that be in Houston? What would Sheridan be doing?

It broke her heart to realize she had no idea what Sheridan's day-to-day normal life looked like. Sheridan knew everything about anything that Lisette did. She knew her routines, her dreams.

Lisette knew Sheridan wanted to be known as the best neurosurgeon in North America, but outside of that? She realized she wanted to know more. She wanted to potentially give Sheridan a second chance. But was she desperate enough for a long-distance relationship?

She knew she wasn't leaving Quebec City. And she doubted Sheridan would leave Houston. Where did that leave them? Long-distance lovers who saw each other a couple of times a year? Was that really what Lisette wanted? Would it be better than the nothing she currently had?

*We should talk.*

It was short and sweet and to the point. The ball was firmly back in Sheridan's court. Would she respond? Only time would tell. Lisette slid her phone in her skirt pocket and went out to see if Gabby needed any help.

She'd barely closed the office door when her phone buzzed. She checked it. Sheridan. Her heart fluttered as she read the text.

*I agree. When? Tonight after work? I could call you around seven your time?*

"Did you text her?" Gabby said.

"Yes. And she just texted back."

"That explains the glow." Gabby smiled.

"Does it now?" But Lisette couldn't fight the warmth that flushed her face. She was talking to Sheridan. Sort of. Well, she would be that night anyway. It had been too long.

*Seven will be great. I look forward to hearing from you.*

"She's going to call me tonight," she said. "I'll be sure and let you know how it goes."

"You'd better."

# CHAPTER TWENTY-THREE

L isette couldn't deny the butterflies as day morphed into evening and seven o'clock approached. She was nervous. She was also excited, and she had to admit it to herself. She wouldn't tell Gabby that in case things didn't go well, but she was holding her breath hoping they did.

At exactly seven, her phone rang. She hadn't changed the ringtone, so when it played, she knew exactly who it was.

"Hello?" Her heart beat a staccato rhythm. She didn't exhale until she heard Sheridan's voice.

"Hi, Lisette."

"How are you, Sheridan?"

"I'm well. How are you?"

"I'm surviving. It hasn't been easy."

"I hear you," said Sheridan. "It's been very hard. Thank you for letting me call you."

Lisette tried to steel herself. She tried to put up roadblocks to her heart. She wanted to keep this conversation all business. She was failing miserably.

"So, you mentioned you'd figured out where the treasure is hidden?" she said.

"I'm like ninety-nine-percent certain. I'd like to fly up next week and go exploring. Would that work for you?"

"Sure. It's cold here now. Just warning you."

"I'll bring warm clothes. Is it cool if I bring Sarah with me?"

"Of course."

"Great. So, um, should I get a hotel? Or?"

"Maybe?" said Lisette. "Oh, Sheridan. I don't know. I don't know what to expect. I don't know how I'll feel seeing you again."

"Hopefully, it'll be like I never left. Maybe we can actually have a conversation about the future instead of being reactive."

"So now I'm reactive?" Lisette was wondering why she'd ever agreed to the phone call.

"No, Lisette. Not you. Us. I'm not proud of how everything went down. I can't speak for you, but I feel like we left things in a state of confusion and miscommunication."

Lisette sighed.

"I suppose you're right. Come up. Stay with me. We can actually talk. About us, about our future."

"I'm glad you're okay with that. I'd very much like a future with you, Lisette."

"Just know I'm not leaving Quebec City."

"Understood," Sheridan said.

What did that mean? Did Sheridan truly understand that? Or was she placating her? Only time would tell.

"Good. I should get going." Though Lisette wanted nothing more than to stay on the phone with Sheridan. All night sounded good.

"Yeah. Me, too. Have a good week and we'll see you Saturday."

"Sounds good. Take care, Sheridan."

"You, too."

The connection was cut. Lisette took deep breaths trying to calm her racing heart. Sheridan was coming back. The future was still murky, but it sounded like at least there would be one.

She was too wired to eat, so she dug into deep-cleaning her house. It was after two when she finally climbed into bed. But she felt good. Great, even. Better than she had in weeks. Sheridan was coming back. That was all that mattered.

"Well?" Gabby said the next morning.

"They'll be back here Saturday."

"That's in a few days. Right on. That's awesome."

"Have you talked to Sarah?" said Lisette.

"Not today. Is she coming too?"

"Sheridan wants her to."

"I'm texting her right now." Gabby pulled out her phone.

"You do that. I'll be in my office."

Lisette finished her bookkeeping and stepped out to talk to Gabby.

"What did Sarah say?"

"She's coming, too. This is going to be epic."

"Oui. I just hope Sheridan really knows where the treasure is buried."

"I have a feeling she does."

"I'm going to step away for a few. I'm going to grab a quick lunch. I'll be back."

Lisette wandered down Rue Ste-Jean. She went into her favorite bistro and had a sandwich and coffee. After lunch, she stopped at a flower shop and bought several bouquets of chrysanthemums. Some purple, some red, some orange. She carried them back to the bookstore. She placed them throughout the store, then made several more trips to pick up more. She was happy with how the store looked and knew Sheridan would appreciate it.

"You're more excited than you're letting on, aren't you?" Gabby said.

Lisette couldn't fight the smile.

"I'm very excited. I have a really good feeling about this weekend."

"So do I. Do you think you and Sheridan will find your happily ever after?"

"I think that's a distinct possibility."

"I'm happy for you," said Gabby. "Really happy for you."

"Thank you. It's scary to allow myself to hope again."

❖

Sheridan picked up Sarah and they were on their way to the airport.

"You ready for this?" Sheridan said.

"I am. You really think you know where the treasure is?"

"I'd bet my bottom dollar on it."

"Excellent."

"Are you looking forward to seeing Gabby?"

Sarah beamed.

"Very much so."

"Good. You sure there's no future for you two?"

"I don't think so. But, as they say, we'll always have Quebec City."

"Yes, you will."

The plane touched down and Sheridan waited impatiently to get off and get their luggage. She planned to get a taxi to take them to the bookstore to see Gabby and Lisette.

As they got to their baggage carousel, Sheridan was surprised to hear her name being called. She turned to see Lisette and Gabby standing there. She engulfed Lisette in a huge embrace while Gabby and Sarah made out like teenagers.

"Guess they're happy to see each other," Sheridan said.

"Not as happy as I am to see you," Lisette said.

"You have no idea how good that is to hear."

"I'm glad. Now get your bags and let's get out of here."

They dropped Sarah and Gabby off at Gabby's place then drove to the bookstore.

"We left Louis in charge," Lisette said. "I'll be more comfortable at the store. We'll head to my place tonight."

"Sounds wonderful." Sheridan was exhausted and would have killed for some alone time with Lisette, but knew it was coming. And that kept her going.

"Are you hungry?"

"I'm actually starving. I have to tell you, I've missed French food."

"Oui. I can imagine. We can have an early dinner. Depending on whether or not Gabby comes back."

"I doubt we'll see either of them until tomorrow," said Sheridan.

"Well then, we'll just check in on Louis then go get dinner. I've been too nervous to eat today."

Sheridan placed her hand over Lisette's.

"Nervous? Why?"

"I didn't know how it would be."

"Seeing me again?"

"Oui."

"I get that," Sheridan said. "I was nervous, too. Then I was just excited."

"I'm glad."

Sheridan squeezed Lisette's hand.

"I'm so grateful you allowed me to come back."

"Could I have stopped you?"

"I don't know. Do you wish you had?"

"No. Definitely not."

The store wasn't very busy, and Louis seemed to have everything under control.

"We're going to get dinner," Lisette said. "I have my phone. Text me if you need anything."

"I appreciate that," said Louis. "But I'm fine. And I'll be fine. You two have fun."

Lisette took Sheridan's hand as they stepped into the cold, bright afternoon.

"I know just the place to take you," she said.

"Is it somewhere we've been before?"

"It is not. It's new to you. But it's one of my favorites."

They sipped wine while they waited for their dinners.

"I'm dying to know," Lisette said. "Where is the treasure buried?"

"I believe it's buried in Lévis."

Lisette's eyes grew wide.

"Are you serious?"

"I am."

"And you're confident about this?"

"*Très.*"

"Oui. You are speaking French now?"

Sheridan laughed.

"I may have picked up a word or phrase from you, but not much. Though, I'm trying to learn. I can say, '*Je veux un chat*.'"

"You want a cat, huh?" Lisette laughed. "That's great though. I'm honored that you're learning my mother tongue."

"I thought it would be nice. I'm really enjoying learning. Though I doubt I'll ever be fluent."

"Well, I appreciate the effort."

After dinner, they strolled back to the bookstore and Lisette let Louis clock out. She and Sheridan stood at the front counter and Sheridan felt undeniable comfort and pleasure at being back in the bookstore. And back with Lisette.

Whatever that meant in the moment, she was fine with. Lisette obviously didn't hate her and that was enough for her. She wondered when she should bring up the future. Would she know when the time was right?

"A penny for your thoughts," Lisette said.

"Oh, I don't know if they're worth that. I'm just thinking about us. Now and what the future might hold for us."

"Sheridan, I don't want to think about the future. It hurt so badly when you left. And now you're back. For how long? Who knows? But I want to simply enjoy the time we have together."

Sheridan didn't know how to feel.

"Do you not think of the future? Do you see yourself with or without me for the time you have left?"

"I don't allow myself to think that far."

"Why not?" said Sheridan.

"As I said, it's too painful."

"What if I wanted to come here? Set up practice? Live in Quebec City? With you? Would you be averse to that?"

"Are you kidding? That would make me the happiest woman on earth. But I couldn't ask that of you."

"What if I'm offering?"

"Sheridan. My God how I hope you're serious. But, for now, let's just be together. See how the next few days play out."

"Are you going to dump me after I find the treasure?" said Sheridan. "Has it all been a game for you?"

"No, Sheridan. Please, don't even joke like that. And don't lose your temper with me. I want a future with you so much I can taste it. But I can't get my hopes up. They were dashed before."

"Before was different. I had patients I'd been putting off. Lifesaving surgeries I'd left in the hands of others. I was being irresponsible and selfish. If you allow me to move here, to be with you, I'll do it the right way. But no decisions have to be made right now."

"Thank you for that." Lisette stood on her tiptoes and kissed Sheridan's cheek. It burned where her lips touched Sheridan's skin. A good burn, though. Sheridan turned and kissed Lisette on the mouth. It was brief and tender, but she hoped it conveyed everything her words didn't.

"That was nice," said Lisette. "I can't wait to close up shop and see what else you have to offer tonight."

"Neither can I."

A group of customers came in then and more followed. They were busy ringing people up and talking books, and the next couple of hours flew by. Finally, Lisette switched the sign on the door to Closed.

"That was fun," Sheridan said. "Like, I had a blast helping people."

"You did very well, too. You're a natural for working with the public."

"I prefer to take people one at a time, if I'm honest."

"I'm sure you're a wonderful doctor. Your patients are lucky to have you."

Guilt creeped into Sheridan's belly as she thought of leaving her patients. It was a very selfish thing to do. But Lisette was worth it, right?

At Lisette's house, Sheridan barely waited until the front door closed to take Lisette in her arms and kiss her with every ounce of pent-up passion she had. Lisette kissed her back in kind and Sheridan's knees were weak as they made their way to the bedroom.

Sheridan took her time undressing Lisette, kissing every new patch of skin exposed. When Lisette stood before her naked, Sheridan quickly stripped and pulled Lisette onto the bed with her. Their lovemaking was frantic, as if neither wanted to take a chance that it was their last time together. Sheridan knew it wouldn't be, but she needed to claim Lisette as hers as quickly as she could.

When they'd each found their release, they fell asleep wrapped in each other's arms. Just before dozing off, Sheridan knew without a doubt, she was home.

## CHAPTER TWENTY-FOUR

Lisette and Sheridan picked up Gabby and Sarah and drove to a restaurant for breakfast.

"We're really going to solve the mystery today?" Gabby said. "This is so cool."

"I sure hope so. I mean, I definitely think so. Or at least discover where it's buried."

"I'm so excited," said Sarah.

"As am I," Lisette said. "I can't believe how close we might be."

They finished their breakfast and got back in Lisette's car.

"Where to?" Lisette said.

"Are you familiar with, and pardon me if I butcher it, but *Église Notre-Dame-de-la-Victoire* Church?"

"I am. I know just where that is. I've even been to Mass there a few times."

"Great. That's where we're heading."

The drive over the St. Lawrence River and into the heart of Lévis took just over twenty minutes. They rode in silence, each lost in her own thoughts about the adventure they were on. And had been on for a while now.

Lisette pulled up in front of a beautiful stone church with a high steeple. Sheridan, who wasn't the least bit religious, was awed by its beauty.

"Let's find where the graveyard is," she said.

Lisette drove around to the back of the church. Grave markers showed they were in the right place.

"Let's do this," said Gabby.

"I didn't realize it would involve grave robbing." Sarah sounded reluctant.

"You can wait here if you need to," said Sheridan.

"I'm with Sarah," Lisette said. "I don't particularly care for cemeteries and graveyards myself."

"Okay," said Sheridan. "Let's look at this on my MacBook. I'll open it on the hood, and you can all see what I've been looking at."

She showed them the map of the church, the graveyard, and the surrounding area.

"Now, look at the map we found in the hidden room."

They all gazed at their phones.

"Do you see what I'm saying?" she said.

"I do," said Lisette. "Wow. You may be right."

"I think I am."

"I'm still waiting in the car," Sarah said. "I'm sorry. I just can't do this."

"It's okay, babe." Gabby kissed her. "We'll be right back."

"Thank you."

They let themselves inside the old, creaky gate and stood among the graves.

"Where do we even begin?" said Lisette.

"I guess we should split up. Look for markers that might say something about Marie Antoinette? Gabby, you take that area over there." Sheridan pointed. "Lisette—"

"I'm staying with you," Lisette said. "No way I'm wandering amongst graves by myself."

"Are you serious? It would save time."

"I don't care. I'm staying with you."

"Okay, then. Gabby, text or call if you find anything."

Some of the markers were well taken care of, but many were in varying states of disrepair. It was hard to make out what they said, but Sheridan didn't give up. She read each headstone and finally came to a section without markers.

"So, you think no one is buried here?" said Lisette.

"Or the ones who were had no one to buy a headstone for them. Or it could be a pauper's grave."

"Don't say that. I don't like the idea that I'm standing on top of a bunch of dead bodies at once."

"This is really freaking you out, isn't it?"

"Yes. Don't you dare make fun of me. I'm still here, freaked out or no."

"Babe, if you want to go back to the car, you can."

"No. If we find the treasure, we do it together."

"Fair enough," said Sheridan.

She began squinting to see writing on aged wooden crosses. Some just had years, others had names.

"I can't believe how old some of these markers are. We're talking centuries old."

"Oui. And now we're disturbing their rest."

"We're not disturbing anybody."

"You don't know that."

They passed under a huge red maple with a few leaves still clinging on for dear life. There were only a few markers in its shade and none of them indicated anything about Marie Antoinette.

"It doesn't seem like many people are buried near this tree," said Lisette. "I wonder why that is. I'd like to be buried under a shade tree."

"Would you? You don't want to be cremated?"

"Dear God, no."

"Really?" Sheridan found this fascinating. "I want to be cremated."

"And where would you like your ashes spread?"

"I don't know. Hopefully, I have a few years to go before I have to decide."

"Oui."

"How old do you think this tree is?"

"It's old. Very old. Hundreds of years old. And it's beautiful," said Lisette.

"Yes, it is.

"I think I'll rest here for a while. Where are you going to look next?"

"I'm going to follow this line up to the church wall. I'll be back in a few."

Lisette leaned against the huge trunk and tried not to think about the fact that she was alone in a graveyard, surrounded by dead bodies with no living soul near her. She felt her pulse race and took some deep breaths to calm herself. She could see Sheridan in one direction and Gabby was slowly moving toward her from the other direction. She was okay. No one could get to her. No one would hurt her.

She took out her phone and studied the map again. Assuming this was the actual spot, where would the X be? She turned her phone vertical to horizontal to vertical again. She was still trying to figure it out when Sheridan came back.

"No joy," she said.

"Me, neither." Gabby joined them. "What are you doing, boss?"

"I'm trying to figure out where the X is. It seems to be right around this tree somewhere but that makes no sense. There aren't many markers right here."

"I'll circle the tree a few times," said Gabby. "Maybe we missed something."

The side door on the church opened and a young priest walked toward them.

"Can I help you with something?" he said.

They looked at each other, not one of them seemingly willing to confess why they were in the graveyard.

"We're admiring this tree," said Sheridan. "It's beautiful."

"Ah, yes. Treasure. That's her name. She's been here for centuries."

"Treasure? Interesting name for a tree," Gabby said.

"There's a story behind it," the priest said.

"We'd love to hear it."

"The story goes like this. After the French Revolution, some expatriates moved to Quebec City with some treasure from the former queen. Wanting to keep the treasure safe, they rowed across the river and buried it here. Then planted the tree so they'd know where it was when they came back for it. But they never did come back."

"What if I told you that wasn't just an old wives' tale?" Sheridan said.

"What do you mean?"

"We found a map in Quebec City depicting a buried treasure. We have done extensive research and were led here. We believe this is indeed where the treasure is buried."

"Mon dieu. You can't be serious."

"We are," said Gabby. "Very. We believe the treasure we search for is somewhere near this tree."

"You must understand. I can't let just anyone start digging. Do you have the map with you? Can you show me?"

"Oui," Lisette said.

Sheridan opened her phone and showed the priest the pictures of the faded map.

"How can you be sure?" the priest said. "This is hard to see and even harder to read."

"Look at the basic outline," said Sheridan. "It's this area of Lévis. And the X? It's definitely the tree."

"It's so hard to see out here. Please, come inside. The light is bright, and I have a magnifying glass."

They followed the priest inside the small chambers off the main church. The little room was well lit, and the priest disappeared down the hall and returned with a magnifying glass.

"Why is the map on your phone? Where is the original map you found?"

"It's in a safe in my office. I own a bookstore in Quebec City," said Lisette. "It's much too fragile to carry around and keep unfolding and folding. Surely you understand?"

"Oui. That makes perfect sense. Okay, let me see this map again."

The priest looked over the pictures of the map on Sheridan's phone. He was silent as he studied them for what seemed an eternity. Sheridan started to get antsy. They were close. So fucking close.

What if the priest decided not to let them dig? What if he didn't agree with them? What would Sheridan do then? Come back at night and dig anyway? She was just about to say something when the priest spoke.

"I have to say I'm inclined to agree with you. It seems like the treasure is indeed buried under the tree. What is the treasure? Do we know?"

"We do not," said Lisette. "Would you claim ownership if it's found here?"

"No. The tree does not belong to the church. It's its own entity. Would the city of Lévis claim ownership? That I don't know."

"They wouldn't if they didn't know about it," Sheridan said.

"Oui. Good point. So, we agree it's buried out there. But we still don't know where. Will you dig up the tree to find it? Or?"

"No, sir," said Lisette. "With your permission, we'll dig around the tree. We'll replace any dirt we displace. We will show the beautiful tree the respect she deserves."

"Very well," said the priest. "I must insist I supervise though."

"That's fine," Sheridan said.

"My name is Raphael, by the way. And you are?"

"My name is Lisette. This is my employee, Gabby, and my dear friend Sheridan."

"Nice to meet you all. I have to say, this is the most exciting thing to happen since I've come to this sleepy town."

Sheridan laughed.

"I don't doubt that."

"Do you need shovels?" Raphael said.

"We brought some. Just in case."

"Great. Then go get them and let's get started."

Gabby and Sheridan left Lisette with Raphael and went back to the car to get shovels.

"What's happening?" said Sarah. "Did you find it?"

"We think so," Gabby said. "There's a gorgeous tree and we believe it's buried by it. The priest told us a story about a buried treasure, so we're almost certain we're in the right place."

"Tree? Priest? Buried treasure? I missed a lot staying in the car."

"You can come with us now," Sheridan said. "The tree is a little removed from most of the graves. You should be okay."

"I don't see that I have a choice. I didn't come all this way to miss out on finding the treasure."

They made their way back to the tree where Lisette and Raphael waited for them.

"Please be careful," Raphael said. "Please do not damage her roots."

"We'll be extremely careful," said Sheridan. "We don't want to hurt her either. She's carried this secret for centuries. We want to see her live for centuries more."

## Chapter Twenty-five

L isette took her shovel from Sheridan and dug the first hole. She dug one shovelful and hit a root.

"Please," said Raphael. "Please be more careful."

"Let's just scoop the dirt off until we know where the roots are," Sheridan said. "They're massive, but we can still do damage if we hit them."

"Excellent idea," Raphael said.

They positioned themselves around the tree and scraped the surface until the roots were exposed.

"Now, let's dig between the roots."

It wasn't long before Lisette's arms and shoulders were aching. She'd always prided herself on being in good shape, but she was in pain. She leaned her shovel against the tree trunk and rested, watching the others continue to dig. Their holes got deeper and wider and still they hadn't found any treasure.

Lisette glanced at Raphael who was wandering among them, making sure they weren't hurting the tree. After a few minutes, Lisette took her shovel and began to dig anew.

She had blisters on her hands. Whose responsibility had it been to bring gloves? Surely, they'd failed. She wanted to cry, but didn't want to cast a gray cloud over the group. So, she gritted her teeth through the pain and dug some more.

She had only been at it for a few minutes when she hit something hard.

"I'm sorry," she said aloud. "I think I hit another root."

Raphael hurried over to her and moved the dirt aside with his hands.

"It's not a root," he said. "It's a box."

The others stopped what they were doing and gathered around the priest on his hands and knees, moving dirt and trying to lift the box out.

"I think you need to dig a little more."

"You're not serious."

"I am."

Lisette looked at her bloody hands before grabbing her shovel.

"I got it, babe," said Sheridan.

She carefully dug under and around the box until Raphael pulled the box out of its hiding place.

"Mon dieu," he said. "I can't believe this is happening."

Lisette's heart pounded. She was a mix of emotions and nerves. She wanted to open the box and see what was in it. On the other hand, she wanted to savor this moment.

The sun was beginning its descent, and she knew they wouldn't be able to see much longer. She made the decision to wait on opening the box.

"Let's put the dirt back," she said. "Let's fill the holes before it's too dark to see what we're doing."

The group walked around the tree, making sure no holes remained, and no roots were left exposed.

"Would you like to come inside and clean up?" Raphael said.

"Thank you so much for the offer," said Lisette. "But I think we need to get home. It's been a long and exciting day."

"If you please," said Raphael. "I'd very much like to know what's in the box."

"I don't blame you," Lisette said. "But we need to figure out how to get the box open."

She handed it to Raphael who ran his hands over the sides and top but could detect no way to open it.

"That's a mystery," he said. "I do hope you figure it out."

"Thank you, Father. For everything. We couldn't have found this without you."

"Lisette, it was my pleasure. Thanks to all of you for brightening my day. I wish you the best of luck."

"And you, Raphael."

Lisette let out an involuntary moan as she picked up her shovel. Sheridan swooped in and took it from her. She threw the spades over her shoulder and walked beside Lisette back to the car.

"How are your hands, oh favorite surgeon of mine?" said Lisette.

"They're not as bad as yours anyway."

"That's good."

They drove back to Lisette's house. She carefully washed off the metal box until they were able to see the cursive R embedded in the front of it.

"Did you bring your signet ring?" Lisette said to Sheridan.

"I did. Let me go get it."

Gabby and Sarah washed their hands and joined Lisette and Sheridan in the dining room.

"This is so exciting," said Sarah. "I'm so glad we came back."

"Me, too." Gabby kissed her.

Sheridan was back with her ring. She handed it to Lisette, who pressed it into the box. It took several tries, but the lock finally gave, and the box popped open.

Lisette carefully lifted out the pouch that was in the box. Whatever was in it had sharp points. What could it be? Lisette set the pouch on the table and opened it gently. She reached her hand in and pulled out a diamond tiara.

There was something else in the pouch. Lisette reached in and pulled out a small vial. She opened it and recognized it immediately as Black Jade, Marie Antoinette's signature perfume.

"Oh, my God," she breathed.

"What?" said Sheridan who reached a hesitant finger out to touch the tiara.

"It's Marie Antoinette's."

"How can you be sure?"

"This is her perfume."

"Seriously?" said Gabby.

"Oui. There's no doubt. It's the same perfume that was with the map."

"This is so cool," Sarah said. "Like, this is a piece of history."

"It really is," said Lisette. "Just think, Marie Antoinette actually wore this."

"What are you going to do with it?" Sheridan said.

"I have no idea. I'm just going to keep it in my safe for a while. Maybe I'll sell it to a museum. Or find her family? Surely someone related to her is still around."

"Wait," Gabby said. "There's something else in the box."

Lisette saw the folded piece of paper. She took it out and read it to the group.

"'Well done. You are now the owner of the tiara that belonged to my beloved queen, Marie Antoinette. It is yours to do with as you see fit. My only request is that it not be given back to the French government.' It's signed Margot and Josephine."

"This is mind-blowing," Sheridan said. "I mean, should we get it appraised?"

"Why?" said Lisette. "I'm not going to sell it yet. And I believe in its authenticity."

Sheridan couldn't help the gnawing at her gut saying it might be a hoax. But why would it be? Who would have gone to all that trouble? And what would it hurt? Lisette believed it was authentic so why rain on her parade? Besides, they had the locket showing Marie Antoinette wearing this same tiara. Sheridan told herself to get a grip and just relax and enjoy the ride.

"Did anyone get Raphael's phone number?" she said. "We should send him pictures."

But not one of them had thought to ask Raphael for his phone number.

"That's okay," said Lisette. "I don't know that I would have trusted even a priest with what was in the box."

Gabby and Sarah left, and Sheridan ordered dinner in. Sheridan could practically feel Lisette buzz with energy. She was so excited and so emotionally high. Sheridan could only smile and try to get her to eat something.

"I'm too excited to eat," Lisette said.

"You need to keep your energy up. Eat something. At least take a few bites."

Lisette finally acquiesced and took a tentative bite.

"This is delicious," she said and proceeded to clean her plate.

Sheridan cleared the table and loaded the dishwasher. She walked back to the dining room, but Lisette had disappeared.

"Where are you?" Sheridan called.

"In here."

Sheridan followed Lisette's voice to the bedroom. The sight that met her made her weak in her knees. Lisette lay naked save for the tiara placed carefully on her head.

"I wish I could take a picture," Sheridan said. "You look amazing."

"Don't you dare."

"I won't."

"Do a striptease for me, Sheridan."

Sheridan laughed.

"That's not going to happen, but I will undress slowly for you to take it all in."

"I appreciate that," said Lisette.

Sheridan removed her sweater and jeans. She stood in her boxers and A-shirt. She was shaking from desire. She wanted to climb on the bed and take Lisette before she got completely naked. She took a step toward the bed.

"No," said Lisette. "I want you naked."

Sheridan quickly removed her undershirt and boxers and climbed onto the bed where she kissed Lisette firmly on the mouth.

"You are so fucking gorgeous," Sheridan said.

"Show me."

"My pleasure."

Sheridan nibbled her way down Lisette's neck until she came to her firm, full breasts. She massaged one while she sucked hard on the other. She took the tip of Lisette's breast in her mouth along with her nipple and ran her tongue all over it while she continued to suck. She loved how long Lisette's nipple grew and how hard it became in her mouth.

She switched to the other breast and did the same. Lisette's hands were in Sheridan's hair, holding her in place.

"Dear God, you make me feel good."

Sheridan didn't reply, simply continued to suckle as though she needed Lisette's breast for survival. She released Lisette's other breast and dragged her hand down her body until she found the heaven where her legs met.

She found Lisette wet and warm and welcoming. Her clit was slick, but Sheridan merely skimmed over it on her way to tease her lower lips and find her entrance. She slid her fingers inside, while her mouth continued to tug and twist Lisette's nipple.

Sheridan was hyper-aroused herself. She shifted her position until her was straddling Lisette's leg. She rubbed herself against Lisette as she thrust deeper and deeper.

Lisette's breathing was coming in hitches. Sheridan knew she was close. Lisette released her grip on Sheridan's head and slid a hand under Sheridan, between her and Lisette's leg.

Sheridan moaned as she rapidly approached her own release. She dragged her fingers out of Lisette and circled her clit. The normally small morsel was swollen in pleasure. Sheridan tried to focus, but she was so close to her own climax that it was very difficult.

She pressed into Lisette's nerve center and rubbed with all the energy she could muster. Lisette helped by arching into Sheridan's touch. Sheridan pressed harder and rubbed faster until her fingers were on autopilot as she took another step closer to the precipice. She barely heard Lisette call her name as she screamed her own pleasure into the night.

When her breathing had returned to normal, Sheridan kissed her way back to Lisette's mouth and she placed a tender peck there.

"Are you going to sleep in that tiara?" she said.

"I'd better not." Lisette removed it and placed it on her nightstand.

Sheridan slept hard that night, grateful to have Lisette in her arms. The mystery had been solved, the treasure found. It was time to figure out what the future held. But that was for another time. That night, all was right in the world.

Lisette woke Sheridan up early. She was between Sheridan's legs and the feel of her tongue on Sheridan was the perfect way to wake up. Sheridan found her release almost immediately. Gone were the days of trying to hold off, to prove what a butch she was. She had nothing to prove with Lisette. And she was so happy they'd found each other.

## CHAPTER TWENTY-SIX

L isette and Sheridan walked into the bookstore to find Gabby and Sarah behind the counter and customers milling about throughout the store.

"Do you have it?" Sarah said.

"Right here." Lisette held up the box. "I'm going to put it in the safe."

"May I ask you a question?" said Sarah.

"Sure."

"Don't you want to try it on? Maybe feel like what it's like to be royalty?"

"She tried it on last night," said Sheridan.

"Did you? How did it feel?"

"It felt amazing," Lisette said.

"May I try it on? Before you put it away?" said Sarah.

"Of course. Gabby, would you like to try it on, as well?"

"No, thanks. Not really my thing."

Lisette unlocked the office door and Sheridan and Sarah followed her. The door closed behind them and Lisette took the tiara out of the box. She handed it to Sarah who placed it gingerly on her head.

"I don't want to break anything."

"You won't. Here, let me help you." Lisette got it positioned properly and stepped back. "Oh, Sarah. You are beautiful. Sheridan, go get Gabby."

Sheridan left and Gabby returned a few moments later.

"Oh, my God. You're gorgeous," she said. She kissed Sarah then stepped back to admire her again. "Absolutely stunning."

Sarah walked over to the mirror and admired herself.

"Someone take a picture, please," she said.

Gabby had her phone out and snapped a few photos.

"I'll send them to you."

"Okay," said Lisette. "I need to put it away now. And Gabby should get back out there in case customers need help."

"On my way." Gabby left the office.

Sarah hung back even after Lisette locked the tiara away.

"What's up, Sarah?"

"I guess it's none of my business, but I have to ask, are you and Sheridan going to stay together this time?"

"That's a very good question. One we haven't touched on, to be honest."

"Well, maybe you should talk about it."

"I'm not leaving Quebec City, Sarah," said Lisette. "And Sheridan has her practice that she won't leave. So, we're kind of at an impasse."

"Are you sure she won't leave her practice?"

"Why would she? Now, if you'll excuse me, I need to get some work done."

Sarah left the office, leaving Lisette alone with her thoughts. Would Sheridan leave her practice? No. She wouldn't. And Lisette wouldn't ask her to. They would simply enjoy what time together they had, and Lisette would protect her heart this time.

She finished with her morning work and left the office. Sheridan and Sarah were at the counter keeping Gabby company.

"Let's go for a walk," Sheridan said.

"You'll freeze." Lisette laughed. "It's only seven degrees outside."

"That's the mid-forties in Fahrenheit. I won't freeze. Trust me."

"I'll let you take me to lunch, then. I'm hungry. Let's walk."

"You're always hungry," said Sheridan. "I'm going to have to get a second job to keep you fed."

Lisette swatted her playfully.

"I do like to eat."

"Mm." Sheridan nudged her. "Thank God."

"Sheridan! We're in public."

"I can still have private thoughts while we're in public."

"I suppose," Lisette said.

They found Lisette's favorite bistro and got in out of the cold.

"It's so cold out there," Lisette said. "But at least it's not snowing."

"Do you get a lot of snow here?"

"Oui. And it's not too early for it, really. We usually get around three meters."

"Wait," said Sheridan. "That's like ten feet. Are you serious?"

"Mm." Lisette sipped her coffee. "It's so beautiful here in the snow. Like a picture postcard. But then it gets old. By March, I've had enough."

"November to March?"

"Sometimes until April."

"Oh, God," said Sheridan. "That sounds brutal."

Lisette's stomach sank. She knew she didn't have a chance of a real relationship with Sheridan, but hearing her response to Quebec's weather pretty much solidified it. She made it perfectly clear she didn't want to live in the snow.

"It's not bad if it's what you've grown up with," she said.

"If you say so."

After lunch, they were walking back to the bookstore.

"That didn't include much of a walk," said Lisette. "You want to walk around for a while?"

"If you won't freeze." Sheridan laughed.

"I won't if you won't."

"Where shall we walk to?"

"Hm. What haven't you seen?"

"You would know better than I."

"Let's check out Porte Saint-Jean," said Lisette. "It's at the entrance to the walled city."

Sheridan took Lisette's hand as they walked. She didn't really care where they went, as long as they were together. Porte Saint-Jean was impressive with its cannons and statues.

The more excited Lisette got telling Sheridan about everything, the thicker her accent got until Sheridan, laughing, had to ask her to slow down. Lisette did and she explained every plaque, every statue in detail. Sheridan thought she would have made a great tour guide if the bookstore gig hadn't worked out.

As they walked back to the bookstore, Lisette said, "That was fun. Did you enjoy it?"

"Very much."

"Good. I love sharing my city with you."

"Good, because I love this city."

"Do you, Sheridan? Do you really?"

Sheridan held her breath, internally begging for Lisette to ask her to move. *Ask me. Please ask me to join you here.* But the offer didn't come.

"So very much," said Sheridan.

"This makes me so happy." She snuggled against Sheridan, who wrapped her arm around Lisette's shoulders and pulled her close. They stopped walking and stood hugging while other pedestrians walked around them.

Sheridan didn't know how long they stood like that. Time stood still. In that moment, everything was perfect. Lisette was pressed against her, and she was in one of the most beautiful cities in the world. What more could she want? An invitation to stay. That would have been the icing on the cake.

Why couldn't Sheridan find the words herself? How hard would it be to tell Lisette she wanted to move here? To tell her she wanted to be in a long-term relationship? That she needed to go back to Houston, but it didn't have to be permanent?

Did she really think Lisette would reject her? Obviously, that's what was holding her back. But why wouldn't Lisette welcome her with open arms? They were so good together.

"As much as I enjoy you holding me, we should get back to the store." Lisette interrupted her musings.

"Oh, yeah. We should do that."

"That was a long lunch." Gabby laughed.

"We went to the Porte Saint-Jean," Sheridan said. "It was really cool."

"Nice."

"Where's Sarah?" said Lisette.

"She's back at my place. She needed a nap."

"Smart lady," Sheridan said.

"Do you need a nap?" Lisette said.

"I may just take one on your couch."

"Perfect. I have work to do in there anyway. Come on."

Sheridan lay as comfortably as she could on the couch. It wasn't designed for her tall frame to lay on, but she'd make it work. She folded an arm over her eyes and started to drift off.

"Merde!" Lisette shouted.

Sheridan woke up, disoriented, but finally focused on Lisette.

"What's wrong?"

"My computer just crashed. Oh, I'm so frustrated."

"I'm sorry. What were you working on?"

"Next year's inventory. I hope I can get my work back."

"I hope so, too. Come here. I'll sit up and I'll hold you until you feel better."

"Don't sit up," Lisette said.

She stood from her desk and crossed the office until she was standing by the couch. Lisette took off her sweater over her head and threw it on the floor.

"What are you doing?" said Sheridan.

"Need you ask?"

She unbuttoned her slacks, lowered the zipper, and stepped out of them. As she stood in her bra and panties, she looked down at Sheridan.

"Shall I continue?"

"Please do."

As Lisette shed her unmentionables, Sheridan worked to get naked on the couch. Lisette straddled Sheridan and the feel of her wet heat on Sheridan's belly had her writhing in anticipation.

"See anything you like?" said Lisette.

"Fuck yes."

Lisette scooted lower until she was straddling Sheridan's upper thighs. Their centers were so close. Sheridan would have killed for a strap-on, but didn't have one, so she relaxed and decided to see what Lisette had in mind.

Leaning back, Lisette supported herself on one arm and used her free hand to lazily run circles around her small clit. Sheridan glanced up at Lisette's face, but her eyes were closed, so she shifted her gaze back to the action. Lisette was leaning in such a way that every inch of her womanhood was on display.

She dragged her fingers along the length of herself before slipping them inside.

"Can you see okay?"

"Oh, yeah." Sheridan finally found her voice.

Lisette slid her fingers out and coated Sheridan's lips with her juices. Sheridan parted her lips and sucked on Lisette's fingers, loving the taste of her woman. Lisette rubbed Sheridan's clit.

"Does that feel good?"

"Oh, dear God, yes."

Lisette repositioned herself and proceeded to rub her own clit while Sheridan's throbbed in annoyance. Lisette slipped her fingers over Sheridan, then over herself. Over and over until Sheridan thought her back would break from arching so high. She was at the edge and needed Lisette to send her over.

Lisette was panting and mewling and Sheridan knew she was on the precipice herself. Lisette's clit had grown significantly, and Sheridan wanted to wrap her lips around it and lick it until Lisette came. But Lisette was in charge and Sheridan watched Lisette's hand rubbing her clit then dipping down to hit Sheridan's.

One, two, three swipes and Sheridan groaned her appreciation as she sailed into oblivion. Lisette shuddered then collapsed onto Sheridan.

"Holy fuck, baby," Sheridan said. "Where in the hell did you learn to do that?"

"I read it in a book once." She blushed. "I just thought it seemed like fun, so I thought I'd try it."

"Well, I'm glad you did."

Sheridan turned Lisette around until she faced away from her.

"Time for dessert," Sheridan said.

She softly licked between Lisette's legs. She knew she'd be tender, but she had to taste her. Sheridan loved Lisette's flavor, but her flavor post orgasm? That was something special.

Soon Lisette was crying out again, finding release in the workings of Sheridan's tongue. Sheridan grinned to herself. Nothing pleased her more than pleasuring Lisette.

As they lay in their post-coital bliss, Sheridan couldn't rest easily. Was this the right time to talk to Lisette about everything that was happening back home? Should she mention how frightened she was in Texas? In her country as a whole?

Lisette jumped up.

"Where's the fire?" said Sheridan.

"We've been in here long enough. They'll be missing us. Get dressed and let's get out front."

Sheridan, realizing her opportunity had passed, reluctantly got off the couch and got dressed. Surely the right time would come again. It had to.

"What about your crashed computer?" Sheridan said.

"Gabby will be able to fix it. I'm sure."

## CHAPTER TWENTY-SEVEN

That night, they met at Lisette's house where Sheridan was making a traditional American dinner. She made meatloaf, mashed potatoes, and peas. Lisette and Gabby had never had meatloaf and, after overcoming their initial hesitance, actually enjoyed it.

The wine was flowing, and everyone was relaxed and enjoying themselves.

"I have to say one thing about you two that I find very different from most Americans I've met," said Lisette. "You guys don't talk about politics a lot."

"The politics of our country are no longer worth discussing," said Sarah.

"I disagree," Gabby said. "I think your politics need to be discussed, called out, and changed."

"I'm not sure there's any hope for change now," Sheridan said. "I think the president-elect is going to abolish the constitution, voting, and everything else that makes our country great."

"I'll confess, I've never paid a lot of attention to your politics on an in-depth level, but he scares me. I've heard things about him." Lisette shuddered.

"Yes. He's a horrible person. And he hates members of the LGBTQ community. Like, with an unhealthy passion," said Sheridan.

"That's why you've got to fight back!" Gabby said.

"To what end?" said Sarah. "He's threatening to lock up protestors."

"Can he do that?" Lisette said.

"He seems to think he can do whatever he wants," said Sheridan. "It's absolutely terrifying."

"Do the states have power? Like individual states? Or does it not work that way?" said Lisette.

"I don't think the states will have any power once he's sworn in. Not that it matters though, Texas is governed by people as twisted in hate as he is."

"Can you move to another state?" said Gabby. "I've heard California is pretty liberal."

"It is, but as I said, I think the national government is going to be set up to override any state laws. I'm really afraid for the U.S."

"I would be, too," Lisette said. "I hope you two remain safe."

"We will," said Sarah. "We don't have any choice."

"Do you really believe he's evil? Or was it all to get elected?" Gabby said.

"He's beyond evil. But he's just the mouthpiece. I believe they'll get rid of him and his vice president will take over. And he's ten times as bad because he actually believes in all the hatred."

"I heard someone compare him to Hitler," said Gabby.

"Yep. I honestly expect to see people rounded up," Sheridan said. "Any minority, any political opponent. Anyone who's a threat to the white male cishet way of life."

"That can't happen," said Sarah. "We have laws."

"Do you think this group cares about laws? I think the first thing they'll do is abolish the constitution."

"Oh, dear God. I hope not," Lisette said.

"I guess we'll just have to see how it plays out, eh?" said Gabby.

"Okay. Enough talk of politics. I'm sorry I brought it up," Lisette said. "Did you make dessert, Sheridan?"

"I sure did. Let's get these dishes cleared and I will serve the apple pie."

"I feel like we should be watching baseball or something," said Sarah.

"Right? Or your American football," Gabby said.

They ate dessert and sipped port and soon everyone was relaxed again. They adjourned to the living room where they played Trivial Pursuit until it was late, and everyone was getting sleepy.

"You two have had a lot to drink," said Lisette. "I don't want you driving, Gabby. The guest room is all made up. I'd appreciate it if you used it tonight."

"I was going to give it a shot, but I think you're right," said Gabby.

"Good call," Sheridan said. "Y'all go tuck in."

"Let me help you with the dishes," said Sarah.

"We will get them," Lisette said. "You are our guests and won't be doing any dishes."

After Sarah and Gabby retired to the guest room, Lisette joined Sheridan in the kitchen.

"You sure know how to make a mess." She laughed.

"I even tried to clean as I went."

"Let's leave these for the morning. Let's go to bed."

"You go to bed. I'll have your kitchen up to snuff in a jiffy."

"I can't go to bed without you," said Lisette. "I'll help."

It took them twenty minutes, but they got the kitchen clean. It was very late or very early depending on which way you looked at it.

"Come on, lover girl," said Lisette. "I have plans for you."

"You have to get up and go to work tomorrow."

"And you're coming with me."

"Why?"

"It's no fair for you to sleep in if Gabby and I have to work."

"Sure, it is." Sheridan laughed.

"Well, regardless, as I said, I have plans for you."

"With Gabby and Sarah just down the hall?"

"I promise to be quiet if you do."

Lisette couldn't get enough of Sheridan. Watching her in the kitchen in her faded jeans and Houston Texans hoodie, she'd wanted to accost her right there. Instead, she'd bided her time, her desire only waxing as the night progressed.

"You need to strip and let me have my way with you," she said.

"What about ladies first?"

"Not tonight. Tonight, you go first. I've kept my hands off you all night. I won't do so any longer. I can't."

She watched as Sheridan slowly and deliberately disrobed. Every inch she bared made Lisette want her more. Lisette had to sit on her hands to keep from ripping Sheridan's undershirt and boxers off herself.

"Now, lay on the bed."

Sheridan lay down and spread her legs. Lisette made short order of her own clothes and with no pretense, climbed between Sheridan's legs.

"Dear God, you're beautiful," Lisette said. "So close to perfection."

She pleased Sheridan with her tongue, lips, and fingers until Sheridan arched her back, let out a guttural moan, and collapsed back on the bed. Lisette kissed her way up to Sheridan's mouth to share her flavor with her.

"Damn," said Sheridan. "Just damn."

She really wanted to close her eyes and just relax in the afterglow, but Lisette was lying naked next to her and that couldn't be ignored. She rolled over and kissed Lisette hard on her mouth. She dragged her hand down her chest to caress and tease her breasts and nipples. She moved it lower until she brought it to where Lisette's legs met.

Sheridan slid her fingers inside Lisette, who let out a low, appreciative moan. Sheridan moved them in and out, over and over, then dragged them over Lisette's swollen nerve center. She circled it slowly, applying more pressure as she did until Lisette bit Sheridan's shoulder which muffled her scream.

"Sleep, my beautiful angel," said Sheridan.

"Oui. Sleep."

It was still dark the next morning when Sheridan awoke to Lisette gently shaking her shoulder.

"Wake up, sleepyhead."

"There's no way."

"If Sarah, Gabby, and I are going to breakfast, then you are, too."

Sheridan rolled over and pulled the covers over her head. She hadn't gotten anywhere near enough sleep and breakfast didn't sound appealing.

"I don't want breakfast," she mumbled.

"Well, you've been outvoted."

Lisette pulled the covers back. Sheridan rolled over to glare at her but stopped when she saw the raw admiration in Lisette's eyes as she gazed longingly at Sheridan's naked body.

"Come back to bed?" Sheridan said.

"Mon dieu! How I wish I could. But the others are getting ready, and you need to, as well."

Sheridan rolled onto her back and spread her legs.

"Are you sure I can't convince you?"

Lisette was silent for a moment as she stared at the heaven between Sheridan's legs. She finally found her voice.

"I want you to get dressed. We're leaving in five."

"Shit."

Lisette left the room and Sheridan, now tired and horny, begrudgingly got out of bed and quickly dressed. She pulled on her 501s, her heavy black cable-knit sweater, thick socks, and warm boots. She hoped she'd be warm enough. This cold climate would be the end of her.

"There she is," Gabby said. "We were beginning to wonder if you went back to sleep."

"I wish," said Sheridan. "What's so important about going to breakfast in the dark?"

"We have to open the store in a few hours. We wanted breakfast before then. Now, wipe that scowl off your face. Let's go," Lisette said.

They went to a little bistro on the other side of town and sat at a table by the fire.

"Last night was so much fun," said Sarah. "We need to do that again."

"Not if it means waking up at oh-dark-thirty the next morning," Sheridan said.

"What are you two going to do today while we work?" said Lisette.

"Sleep," Sheridan said.

"Have another cup of coffee, grumpy," Lisette said.

"Have three or four." Gabby laughed.

"I'm working on it. Sarah, what do you want to do?"

"I have no idea. Is there anything we haven't seen yet?"

Lisette said, "Probably. There's so much to see and do here."

"You guys haven't seen the falls yet, have you?" said Gabby.

"No," Sarah said. "You want to do that today, Dr. Rousseau?"

"Sure. That sounds like a great way to freeze my ass off."

Lisette playfully swatted Sheridan's arm.

"Okay," Sheridan said. "I'll lose the 'tude. The falls sound wonderful."

"Yay," said Sarah.

They finished breakfast and dropped Lisette and Gabby at the bookstore. Sheridan drove Lisette's car out to the Montmorency Falls.

"Damn," said Sheridan. "These are impressive."

"I read that they're even higher than Niagara Falls."

"No shit? They're gorgeous. That's for sure."

While they were out and about, Sarah suggested they visit Ste-Anne-de-Beaupré, which was a town not far from the falls. Just as they pulled into town, a few fat flakes fell from the sky.

"Snow?" said Sheridan. "We're going to freeze."

"It's beautiful, though, don't you think?"

"Yeah. From inside a warm car. It better not seriously snow, or we'll be stranded. I've never driven in the snow, Sarah."

"Should we turn around and head back?"

"I think we should."

On the drive back to Quebec City, Sarah broached the subject Sheridan had been trying to avoid.

"Have you talked to Lisette yet?" said Sarah.

"About?"

"Moving here?"

"Sarah," said Sheridan. "I don't know that she wants me here. I think this is just fun and games for her."

"That's not what Gabby says."

"What does Gabby say?" Sheridan asked, against her better judgment.

"That Lisette was absolutely devastated when we left last time. She had to be reminded to eat. There were even a couple of days she didn't come into the store."

"Wow."

"Yeah. Does that sound like fun and games to you?"

"No. It definitely does not."

"So, talk to her," said Sarah.

"I keep thinking of bringing it up, but it never seems to be the right time."

"Well, we're supposed to go back soon, so I suggest you do it at the earliest opportunity."

## CHAPTER TWENTY-EIGHT

The next morning, Sheridan and Lisette made love then Lisette took her shower to get ready for work. She was surprised to see Sheridan was still awake when she walked back into the bedroom.

"What are you doing? I thought you'd be sound asleep." She laughed.

"We really need to talk, babe."

A sinking feeling crept through Lisette's body, but she fought not to show it.

"About?" She continued to face the closet, faking concentration on her clothes.

"Why don't you come over here and sit down on the bed?"

"Sheridan, I've got to be honest. You're scaring me." But she sat on the bed.

"My vacation here is almost up," said Sheridan.

"Yes. Unfortunately, I'm aware of that."

"I have to go back to the States."

"Yes."

"I'd like to come back here."

"You're always welcome. You know that," Lisette said.

"That's not what I mean."

"Then what do you mean?" Lisette fought tears. What else could Sheridan be talking about? Did she not want to come visit Lisette? The hurt was palpable.

"Lisette, I'm crazy about you. You must know that."

"Are you? Then what are you saying?"

"That I want to be with you. Like, in a relationship. Together."

Lisette sighed.

"Sheridan, you know I don't want to do a long-distance relationship. I care about you. Deeply. But I won't be in a relationship with someone thousands of miles away."

"So, what if I moved here?"

"You're funny. You have a life there. You're a doctor. With patients who need you."

"I could open a practice here. It would take some work, but I could do it," said Sheridan. "I'm internationally known. I'm sure Canada wouldn't mind having me here."

"I'm still not sure I understand."

"I'm asking if you'd like me to move in with you. You're not making it easy, so I'm guessing that gives me my answer."

Sheridan got out of bed, went into the bathroom, and slammed the door behind her. Lisette sat on the bed, stunned. It was as if her every dream was coming true. Was it possible? Dare she hope? Was Sheridan serious? She needed to find out.

"Sheridan? Please come out of there. We need to discuss this seriously."

The bathroom door opened, and Sheridan stood in the frame.

"Is it something you're interested in?" she said.

"It is. I mean, if you mean it?"

"I do."

"Oh, Sheridan!" She wrapped her arms around Sheridan's neck. "Oh, yes, Sheridan. Please make it happen."

Sheridan kissed Lisette hard on her mouth and they fell backward onto the bed. Hands searched, fingers probed, tongues frantically lapped at each other until they both lay back, breathing heavily.

"Damn. What you do to me," said Sheridan.

"Tell me about it. Mon dieu."

"So, you'd really be okay with me moving in? Or would you rather I get my own place for a while?"

"I'd love for you to live with me. Just think, all the sex we could handle, waking up together every day, going to sleep holding each other every night."

"It does sound like heaven, doesn't it?"

"Oui. It truly does," Lisette said. "But tell me, logistically, how long until that comes true?"

Sheridan propped herself on an elbow and looked into Lisette's eyes.

"I honestly don't know. It shouldn't be that long. I have to let my practice know. They'll take care of making sure my patients are distributed. I'll need to inform the Texas Medical Board and, of course, my patients. I can post it on my website and in my office. And, naturally, we'll do a mass mailing to let my patients know. I don't know the actual timeframe, but I'm thinking months if not sooner."

"That is fantastic. I've heard scary things about Texas

"I just need to notify my patients and partners. I'm not asking permission."

"Oh, good. Wouldn't it be wonderful if we could bring in the New Year together?"

"It would be fucking amazing. But let's not get ahead of ourselves. I have a lot to do to get ready. Plus, I need to see about practicing here," said Sheridan.

"True. Do you know what that entails?"

"Not a clue. I may actually just apply for a teaching position at the university. But I think I'd be more useful actually practicing. We'll figure it out."

"Oh, Sheridan, I'm so excited. You've made me the happiest woman on earth."

"Good. I'm pretty fucking happy myself."

"We need to tell the others," Lisette said.

"True. I should probably talk to Sarah first though. This announcement will have ramifications for her, you know?"

"Oui. This is very true. I hadn't thought about that. Well, you do that while I go to work. I'll tell Gabby the good news while you tell Sarah."

"Sounds good."

Sheridan kissed Lisette goodbye and took her shower and dressed. She sent Sarah a text asking if she was up for breakfast. After Sarah agreed, Sheridan called a taxi to take her to the restaurant.

Sarah was waiting for her when she arrived.

"Hey, boss. How are you this morning?"

"I'm wonderful, and you?"

"Wonderful? That must be nice. What's got you in such a good mood?" said Sarah.

"Well...I talked to Lisette this morning."

"About?"

"Moving here."

"Oh, wow. How'd that go?"

"It went very well," Sheridan said. "I'll be notifying everyone as soon as we get back. Then we'll go about moving my patients around."

"Oh, wow, Dr. Rousseau. I'm so happy for you. That's fantastic."

"Thank you, Sarah. I'm very excited. But we need to figure what will happen to you."

"I'm sure I could work for one of the other doctors. I mean, I think I've proven myself so one of them should pick me up. Don't you think?"

"I don't see why not. If that's truly what you want?"

"Of course. I love my job," said Sarah.

"Great. Then I'll do what I can to make that happen."

"Thank you. I appreciate that. I'm really going to miss you. You're a great boss."

"So...what about Gabby?"

"What about her?"

"Will you do the long-distance thing?" Sheridan said.

"Oh, I don't know. I mean I really like her, but I don't think she's playing for keeps."

"Have you asked her?"

"Of course not. I'm trying to keep things free and easy. Just how she likes it."

"I think you need to ask yourself how you like it. Do you want it free and easy? Or do you want a relationship?" said Sheridan.

"I don't really have time for a relationship. I'm pretty much married to my job."

"That's not what I asked."

"Whatever," said Sarah. "Let's just finish our breakfast and get to the bookstore. I'm sure you're excited to tell Gabby."

"Lisette is taking care of that. But finish up so we can go there anyway."

They ate as much as they could, Sheridan paid the tab, and they hailed a taxi to take them to Rue Ste-Jean and the bookstore. Gabby was all smiles when they walked in.

"Congrats, Sheridan. I'm so happy for you," she said.

"Thank you. I'm pretty happy for me, too."

"I'm sure."

"Is Lisette in the office?"

"Yeah, but she should be out soon."

"Excellent," said Sheridan. "I'll go find a book."

"Actually, can you do me a favor?" said Gabby.

"Sure. What's up?"

"I need to run a quick errand. Would you two mind watching the place until Lisette comes out?"

"Sure." Sarah looked confused. "I think we can handle it. Do you want some company?"

"Thanks, but it'll only take me a minute. Thanks, you two." She kissed Sarah then ran out the front door.

"She's acting weird," said Sarah.

"She probably forgot to do something this morning and wants to get it taken care of before Lisette finds out."

"Maybe."

"Relax. Seriously. What else could it be?" Sheridan said.

"I don't know. Just a feeling I get. Something is off."

Lisette came out of her office. Sarah enveloped her in a bear hug.

"I'm so happy for you," she said. "You and Dr. Rousseau make such an awesome couple."

"Thank you," said Lisette. "I'm just thrilled that Sheridan wants to get serious. My heart got involved a long time ago, but I didn't have any clue she felt the same."

"She does," Sarah said. "Believe me."

"Thanks for the help, Sarah, but I think I've got this," said Sheridan.

Lisette laughed.

"Where's Gabby?"

"She said she had to run an errand," Sheridan said.

"That's strange. I can't imagine what errand she needed to run."

"Right?" said Sarah.

"Relax." Sheridan looked at Lisette. "Sarah is trying to come up with all kinds of conspiracy theories."

"I can't really blame her."

"You two are going to drive me to drinking."

"Speaking of drinking," said Lisette. "I have a leftover bottle of champagne in my office. Who wants to celebrate?"

"What's it left over from?" said Sarah.

"Some party. I don't remember."

"Champagne sounds wonderful," said Sheridan. "We are indeed celebrating."

"Let me go find it. Sheridan, would you mind going and buying some ice?"

"On my way."

Sheridan stepped out into the bitter cold and looked both ways. Where was the nearest spot to purchase ice? She remembered a liquor store a little way up the street, so headed that direction. She put her head down against the biting wind and forged onward.

She bumped into someone.

"Sorry."

"Sheridan?"

Sheridan looked up.

"Gabby."

"Where are you going?"

"To get ice?"

"Why?"

"We're drinking champagne to celebrate."

"Excellent. I'll see you there."

Sheridan stepped gratefully back into the warm bookstore with a bag of ice.

"I wasn't sure how much we need."

"Just enough to chill the bottle," said Lisette. "I'll pour the ice in the sink and cool the champagne."

"What errand were you running?" Sarah said to Gabby.

"Hm? Oh, nothing major. Just something I'd been putting off. I decided today was the day."

"I'm very curious," said Sarah.

"Really? Why?"

"I don't know."

"She's suspicious of you." Sheridan laughed.

Lisette joined them.

"Champagne is cooling. What shall we do while we wait?"

"We can go into the office and make out," said Sheridan.

"Or you could watch the counter while Sarah and I borrow your office."

"Such choices." Lisette laughed. "How about we all stay here until the champagne is ready. It shouldn't take that long."

"Fine," said Gabby.

A group of customers approached to pay for their finds. Gabby helped them while the other three moved to the side so they wouldn't interfere.

"You know, Sarah, if you moved here, I'd hire you in a heartbeat," said Lisette.

"You're too kind. But I don't see myself moving here."

"What are you going to do then?"

"I'll work for one of the other doctors. I love my job and, while it won't be the same without Dr. Rousseau, it'll still be an amazing job."

The customers cleared out and Sheridan heard music playing from Gabby's Mac. It was Lionel Richie. He was singing "Three Times a Lady." Sheridan realized the others heard it too. She glanced at Gabby who was staring at Sarah. Gabby was singing along. She was singing to Sarah.

Sarah was watching Gabby, tears in her eyes. Gabby came around from behind the counter and took Sarah's hands. She continued singing until the song ended.

"I do love you," she said. "And I'd like you to be my girlfriend. Will you?"

"Are you serious?"

"I am. I'd rather it be here, but even if it's in Texas, I don't give a fuck. I want you to be mine."

She slipped a rainbow ring on Sarah's finger. Sarah was sobbing and laughing and nodding.

"Yes, Gabby. Oh, dear God, yes."

"Champagne for everyone," cried Lisette.

## CHAPTER TWENTY-NINE

By the time Louis showed up for his shift, nobody was feeling any pain. Lisette offered him some champagne, but he declined. He took over the counter and Lisette and the others moved the celebration into Lisette's office.

"We should be partying in the secret room," said Gabby.

"Excellent idea," Lisette said. "Let's go down there."

"We need more champagne," said Sheridan. "I'll meet y'all down there."

"We'll go get champagne," Gabby said. "Come on, Sarah."

They left and Lisette opened the stairway down to the secret room.

"Come on, my love. Let's go."

She led Sheridan downstairs where she saw the sleeping bag still on the floor. Memories of their last trip down there flooded her. That was the day Sheridan had left. She calmed her nerves and reminded herself that, although Sheridan would be leaving again, she would eventually come home. To her.

"I remember our last trip down here." Sheridan took Lisette in her arms. Lisette felt immediately comforted and aroused.

"Do you think we have time?"

Sheridan laughed.

"I don't know about that. But maybe we can have a heavy make out session?"

"Mm. That sounds nice. A little promise of things to come?"

"Yes, lover. Things to come for sure."

Lisette looked into Sheridan's amazing violet eyes and melted. She saw everything in those eyes. Passion, admiration, love? Dared she dream? Mostly she saw home. She knew, no matter what happened, Sheridan would always be home.

There was a small loveseat along one wall. Lisette took Sheridan's hand and guided her over to it.

"Will this even support us?" Sheridan said. "How old is it?"

"Your guess is as good as mine. Let's try. Please?"

She sat on the loveseat and pulled Sheridan down with her. Apparently satisfied it would support them, Sheridan pulled Lisette close and kissed her hard on her mouth. Lisette melted into Sheridan and kissed her back with all the passion coursing through her.

They continued kissing while Sheridan's hands roamed all over Lisette's body. She slipped her hand up inside Lisette's sweater and Lisette moaned into Sheridan's mouth. Sheridan squeezed and teased her nipples and soon all Lisette wanted was to feel Sheridan inside her.

Lisette hiked up her skirt and grabbed Sheridan's arm.

"Touch me," she whispered.

"You two decent down there?" Gabby's voice broke through Lisette's delirium. She sat up, got her clothes put back together, and called back.

"We are. Come on down."

Gabby and Sarah came down with four more bottles of champagne.

"Dear God, we're going to be blitzed," said Sheridan.

"That's the goal," Gabby said.

"Come on, let's fill our glasses and make some toasts," Sarah said.

They toasted to each other, to Quebec City, to the future, and to treasures sought and found.

"So, Sarah," Lisette said. "Sheridan is coming back here. Are you coming, too? Or are you two going to do the long-distance thing?"

"We haven't decided yet."

"But you would like to live here, oui?"

"Yes. I would. It would be safer and makes the most sense. But I have family and friends in the States. It's a hard call."

"We will last however long it takes," said Gabby. "Eventually we'll be together. That's what's important."

"Are you considering moving to Houston?" Lisette said.

"No. Not now. We'll see though."

"I think we'll all end up here. In this gorgeous city with our gorgeous women," said Sheridan.

"I'll drink to that," Gabby said. "You know what we need to do? We need to dance."

She went upstairs and returned moments later with her MacBook.

"I'm taking requests. What do we want to hear?"

"Disco," said Lisette.

"Donna Summer?"

"Oui! Play it loud."

They danced and danced and moved and grooved all over the little room. Donna Summer accompanied them as they gyrated with each other. A slow song finally came on and they moved into each other's arms. Their dancing soon morphed into kissing each other and soon Lisette was tired of waiting for Sheridan.

"I think I've had enough," she said. "We should head home."

"The day is young," said Gabby.

"Oui, but I'm tired. Eventful day and champagne and now I'm sleepy. I need a nap."

"Crash on the couch in your office for a few then join us again."

Sheridan piped up, "I agree. We should go home and nap. Let's plan on meeting later for dinner?"

"Sounds good," said Sarah. "Can we stay down here?"

"Of course," Lisette said. "Enjoy yourselves."

They took a taxi since Lisette was in no shape to drive. Sheridan and Lisette made out like teenagers in the back of the cab. The cabbie didn't seem to mind. He ignored them until he had to break them up to tell them they had arrived at Lisette's house.

Lisette fumbled with the keys to get in but finally got the door open. They closed it behind them and began making out again. They were too entwined to go far so Sheridan eased Lisette onto the closest couch and climbed on top of her.

Lisette pulled her skirt up again and slid her panties down. She rested her knees on Sheridan's shoulders and Sheridan immediately got the hint. She took Lisette in her mouth and Lisette groaned gratefully. Sheridan worked magic with her tongue and lips and soon Lisette was screaming as the orgasms cascaded over her.

Sheridan stood on shaky legs and stripped. She looked down at Lisette, still spread-eagle on the couch and wondered if she'd ever tire of making love to her. As she stood looking down, she absentmindedly stroked herself.

"Hey now," murmured Lisette. "Let me have some of that."

Sheridan lay on top of Lisette who immediately found her center with her fingers. She probed and rubbed and coaxed one climax after another out of her. Sheridan lay spent. She was satiated and with the woman she loved.

That thought woke her right up. Did she love Lisette? Like, truly love her? Or was this deep infatuation? She didn't want to examine it too much, but now that she was thinking about it, she was forced to. And what if she did love her? Did Lisette love her too? Should she tell Lisette she loved her? What if Lisette laughed in her face? Surely, she wouldn't. Or would she?

"Baby?" said Lisette. "Let's go to bed. We can sleep and make love again later."

Lisette quickly shed her clothes, leaving them in a pile on the couch. Sheridan followed behind, her stomach a knot of nerves. But the sight of her naked body caused other reactions, which overrode her nerves.

She *did* love Lisette, and she needed to tell her. She lay next to Lisette on the bed.

"Hey, babe?"

"Mm?" Clearly Lisette was already dozing.

"There's something I need to tell you."

Lisette opened her eyes and looked at Sheridan.

"What is it? Is everything okay?"

"I think so. I don't know. That's up to you."

"You're scaring me again. What's on your mind? Just say it."

Sheridan rolled over until she was on top of Lisette. Flesh to flesh, eyes looking into each other, Sheridan knew she was doing the right thing.

"Lisette?"

"Yes?"

"I love you." Sheridan watched the tears leak out of Lisette's eyes and slide into her hair. "Babe? Say something."

"Mon dieu, Sheridan. You make me the happiest woman on earth. I love you, too. So very much."

"Tell me in French."

"J'taime."

"Now it's official." Sheridan kissed Lisette gently on her lips, but the kiss soon morphed into something carnal. Raw desire and need coursed through her and she had to have Lisette again.

She ran her hand down Lisette's body until she came to where her legs met. Sheridan found her wet and warm and ready for her. She gently entered her with two fingers and Lisette opened her legs wider.

"More, please," said Lisette.

Sheridan was happy to oblige. She could feel Lisette's juices spilling onto her wrist and knew how delicious she would taste. She kissed down Lisette's body until she could lap at her juices and run her tongue over her tiny nerve center. She felt Lisette's hand on the back of her head, pressing her into her and holding her in place.

Not that Sheridan needed that. She wasn't going anywhere. She was in her happy place, and nothing could tear her away. She continued to enjoy Lisette until Lisette stiffened, cried out, and collapsed back onto the bed.

This didn't stop Sheridan. She replaced her fingers with her tongue and lapped up the remnants of Lisette's orgasms.

"No more," Lisette whispered. "Sleep time."

Sleep was the last thing Sheridan wanted. Her body hummed with desire that only Lisette could quench. But Lisette was already breathing softly indicating she was down for the count.

Sheridan had options. She knew this. She could wait until Lisette awoke, or she could take matters into her own hands. Or both. She went into the bathroom for privacy and eased the ache inside her.

Lisette woke Sheridan up some time later by licking and sucking between her legs.

"Oh, damn baby. What you do to me," Sheridan said.

"Mm."

Sheridan moved her hips up and down in time with Lisette's tongue until her world burst into colors and she rode the waves that crested inside her. She didn't think she'd ever been with a more talented lover, and she was absolutely thrilled that she'd be with her forever.

"We need to get ready for dinner," Lisette said.

"You just ate."

"Very funny. Come on, stud. We need a shower."

"Tell me you love me again."

"J'taime."

"Yes. I love you, too."

Sheridan devoured Lisette in the shower before finally settling in to get clean. After, when they were dried and dressed, Sheridan texted Sarah to see if they still wanted dinner.

Sarah responded that they'd spent the afternoon much the same way Sheridan and Lisette had, but they'd be ready for dinner in twenty minutes. They agreed on a restaurant and Sheridan turned her attention back to Lisette, who looked stunning in black jeans and a green tunic sweater.

"Let's skip dinner and stay in and have dessert," said Sheridan.

"Very funny. Didn't you get enough in the shower?"

"I'll never get enough of you, Lisette. Never."

"You are so sweet."

"I'm honest."

"Well, you're honestly sweet," Lisette said.

They met Sarah and Gabby and ordered more champagne to celebrate.

"So, what does moving here look like for you?" Gabby said. "What do you have to do? Like, for your practice?"

"I'll have to jump through some hoops. It shouldn't be bad, though. Should be pretty simple. I'm more concerned with opening a practice here, if I'm honest."

"They'll be lucky to have you," said Sarah.

"Well, thank you. And maybe once I'm established here, you can come work for me again."

"That would be amazing."

"We'll be all set then."

"So, does this mean you're moving to Quebec City, Sarah?" said Lisette.

"I think it does."

"Yay." Gabby kissed Sarah.

"We need to go dancing after dinner," Lisette said.

"Do we though?" said Sheridan.

"Yes!"

Sheridan laughed.

"Fine, but where?"

"I know just the place," said Gabby. "Let's get out of here."

# EPILOGUE

*Five Years Later*

Sheridan finished with her last patient of the day. It was just past six and she was exhausted. Sarah poked her head in Sheridan's office.

"How you doing, Dr. Rousseau?"

"I'm wiped. How are you?"

"About the same." Sarah laughed. "But Gabby wants to go out tonight and we wondered if you and Lisette wanted to join us?"

"What time?"

"Well, we want to go dancing, but if you and Lisette would be up for dinner and drinks, that would be fun."

"Where?"

"We haven't made it that far." Sarah laughed again. "But I'll text you when we decide, and you can choose to join us or not."

"Sounds good. Don't wait too long though. I'm starving and exhausted, which is not a good combo."

"Not good at all. I'll text you before you even get home. I promise."

Sheridan drove to her house. It was so nice to think of it as hers now. For the first few years, she'd continued to refer to it as Lisette's house. But it was hers. Hers and Lisette's. The thought made her smile.

She had never been happier than she had since moving to Quebec City. Lisette's bookstore continued to thrive, and Sheridan had built a nice practice. She spent her days working hard and her nights in Lisette's arms. What more could she ask for?

Sheridan saw Lisette's car in the driveway. She loved coming home to Lisette. It didn't always happen that Lisette got home first, but Sheridan was happy when she did. She opened the door.

"Mrs. Rousseau? Are you home?" Sheridan called.

"I am." Lisette walked to the entry hall with a glass of wine in one hand and a glass of tequila in the other. She handed the tequila to Sheridan then kissed her. "Welcome home."

"Mm. Thank you. The girls want to go out for dinner and drinks. Are you up for that?"

"Sure. Are you?"

"Ugh," said Sheridan. "Not really, but I'm sure I'll feel better once I get some food in my stomach."

"Yes. What is the word you use? Hangry?"

Sheridan laughed.

"That is indeed the word."

"Where do they want to meet? And when?" said Lisette.

Sheridan showed her Sarah's text with the restaurant's name that she couldn't pronounce. Not for lack of trying. Sheridan spent hours trying to learn French, but she couldn't seem to grasp it. Even with Lisette's patient assistance.

"Oui," Lisette said. "It won't take long to get there. Do you want to change?"

"No. I'm good." She downed her tequila in one gulp. "I'm ready when you are."

"I'll put my wine in the fridge. Then we can go."

"I'll call a taxi. I want us both to relax and have fun. No driving."

"Good idea, my wise wife."

Sheridan was Lisette's wife. It still struck her as surreal. They'd gotten married three years earlier and, while nothing had technically changed, it just made everything better knowing Lisette was her spouse.

They arrived at the restaurant that had a bohemian chic vibe. Sheridan felt immediately at ease, and they quickly found Sarah and

Gabby in the bar area. Lisette let out a squeal when she saw Sarah and quickly engulfed her in a hug.

"Mon dieu. I'm so happy for you," she said.

"What am I missing?" said Sheridan.

Lisette stepped back and held up Sarah's left hand. There sat a solitary diamond.

"Does this mean what I think it means?" said Sheridan.

"It does," said Gabby. "We're going to make it official."

"Outstanding. Congratulations." Sheridan shook Gabby's hand and hugged Sarah. "I'm so happy for you both."

"When's the big day?" said Lisette.

"We haven't gotten that far." Gabby laughed. "I'm just glad she said yes."

"She would have been a fool not to," said Sheridan.

"I agree," Sarah said.

They ordered drinks and Lisette and Sarah launched into a discussion about wedding gowns while Gabby and Sheridan just hung out pretending not to be interested.

"You're going to be a gorgeous bride," said Lisette. "I can't wait to see you on your special day."

"Can I talk to you for a minute, Dr. Rousseau?" Sarah said.

"Sure. What's up?"

"Let's get a table. And you may want another drink."

"Uh-oh. Are you quitting?"

"I'm not quitting. I just have a favor to ask of you," said Sarah.

Sarah bought Sheridan another tequila then joined her at a table at the other end of the bar.

"What's up?" Sheridan said.

"Dr. Rousseau?"

"You know, when we're not at work, you can call me Sheridan. I do believe I've mentioned that about a thousand times now."

"I know. But it feels disrespectful."

"Suit yourself. Anyway, how can I help?"

"I was wondering…"

"Yes?"

"Would you mind giving me away? At the wedding, I mean?"

Sheridan couldn't believe her ears. She sat staring at Sarah in disbelief.

"Sarah, it would be my honor to give you away," she said.

"Oh, thank you." Sarah got up and hugged Sheridan. "Thank you so much."

"Of course. It's an honor and a privilege. I'm so happy you asked."

"Me, too."

They joined the others again.

"That didn't take long," said Lisette.

"Nope. Dr. Rousseau is the best."

"You look quite proud of yourself, babe," Lisette said. "What on earth is that cocky grin all about?"

Sarah looked at Gabby.

"She said yes."

"Oh, Sheridan," said Gabby. "Thank you so much. I know how much this means to Sarah."

"My pleasure."

"Does someone want to tell me what's going on?"

"I asked Dr. Rousseau to give me away," said Sarah.

"Mon dieu. That is exciting."

"Right?" Sheridan said.

They finished their drinks and headed to the dining room where the conversation about the wedding continued. By the time dinner was over, a date had been set for that summer. The venue was still up in the air, though they all agreed a small wedding would be better than a big spectacle.

"I had an announcement to make, too. Though not quite as exciting," said Lisette.

"Do tell," Sheridan said.

"I found some time today to finally look into the mysterious Josephine and Margot."

"Seriously?" said Gabby. "That's awesome. What did you learn?"

"Well, from what I could figure out, Margot and Josephine were lovers. Josephine was in Marie Antoinette's court."

"Oh, wow," Sarah said.

"And Josephine's last name?"

"The suspense is killing me," said Sheridan.

"Yeah. Spill it. What was her last name?"

"Rousseau."

"No shit?" Gabby said.

"It's the truth. It's taken a lot of digging. But that's what I've come up with."

"That is way cool. That explains why Sheridan's ring opened the box," said Sarah.

"Oui. They must be relatives."

"I knew I had an ancestor in her court, but wow. Just wow."

"So now all the mysteries are solved," said Lisette.

In the taxi on the way back to their house, Lisette snuggled up against Sheridan.

"You're such a good person, Dr. Rousseau."

"I'm glad you think so, Mrs. Rousseau."

"Mm. I do. I'm sure it means the world to Sarah that you're going to give her away. And, on a personal level, I can't wait to see you in a tux again."

"Is that right? Well, I can't wait to see you naked, so there's that."

"Sheridan!" She slapped her arm and looked toward the driver who seemed oblivious. Sheridan just laughed.

Back in their house, Lisette asked Sheridan if she wanted another drink.

"All I want is you, baby."

"Well, I'm all yours for the taking."

"I do like the sound of that."

They walked to the bedroom where Lisette quickly undressed and climbed into bed. There she lay watching Sheridan strip. The sight of Sheridan's naked body never ceased to arouse her. Even after all these years together. Naked Sheridan made her quiver.

Sheridan slid into bed beside her, and all was right in Lisette's world. Sheridan gently kissed Lisette's eyelids, nose, and finally, her lips. Lisette opened her mouth, and Sheridan slipped her tongue inside.

They kissed for what seemed an eternity until Lisette's hips began pumping of their own accord. She arched into Sheridan, craving her touch. Sheridan didn't seem to have the same sense of urgency.

She kissed down Lisette's neck and nibbled her shoulders.

"Mon dieu, Sheridan. Please."

Sheridan kissed Lisette's chest and finally took a nipple in her mouth. Lisette felt lightning course through her as she arched off the bed. The lightning hit hard between her legs, and she knew she was close. She just needed Sheridan to seal the deal.

Sheridan finally touched Lisette's most private parts and tenderly entered her.

"Oh," Lisette gasped. She took Sheridan's hand and placed it on her clit. She held her there and together they rubbed her into oblivion. The orgasm was quick and powerful, and just what Lisette needed.

"My needy baby," said Sheridan.

"That would be me."

Sheridan moved until she was between Lisette's legs. She took Lisette in her mouth. Lisette bucked on the bed, riding Sheridan's talented tongue. She lost herself in the feelings. Eyes closed, every muscle tensed in anticipation, she let herself just feel until she felt the ball of heat in her very center explode and shoot the warmth throughout her body.

She felt complete, as she always did after Sheridan made love to her. It was a feeling that she hadn't ever known and could now not imagine living without. Sheridan finished and lay next to Lisette.

"You are amazing. There are no words," said Lisette.

"I'm glad you think so. There is no greater pleasure for me than making you come."

"Well then, it's wonderful for both of us. Now, you lie back and let me have my way with you."

"I thought you'd never ask."

Lisette threw the covers off Sheridan and took her place between her legs. She lightly ran her fingers over Sheridan, admiring her sheer perfection.

"Whenever you're ready," said Sheridan.

"You're just so beautiful. You're absolutely perfect. I don't even know where to start."

"Start anywhere. Just start. Please."

Lisette didn't need to be asked again. She buried her fingers inside Sheridan and took her swollen clit in her mouth. She ran her tongue over it and sucked on it while she plunged her fingers deep over and over.

Sheridan arched off the bed, froze, cried out, then collapsed in a heap.

"Damn, baby," she said.

"Mm."

Lisette curled up against Sheridan. Everything was right in her world. Sheridan's arm was around her, holding her tight. She was right where she belonged.

The next morning, Lisette was up early getting ready to go to work. It was Saturday, but it was a new month, so she had month-end duties to attend to. After she was dressed, she looked longingly at Sheridan, still fast asleep. She wanted to get undressed and join her but didn't. She had work to do and Sheridan would be there when she got home. Sheridan would always be there. She would never be alone again.

# About the Author

MJ Williamz grew up on California's Central Coast. It was there that their teachers, starting in fifth grade, encouraged them to pursue writing as a career. Their writing took off in the environment of Portland in the Pacific Northwest. In 2014, they married fellow Bold Strokes Book author Laydin Michaels. The move to Houston to be with Laydin was just what MJ needed to continue writing. MJ now lives in Puerto Vallarta with their dog, Zeus. They can't wait for Laydin and the rest of the gang to join them.

# Books Available from Bold Strokes Books

**Chasing Her Scent** by MJ Williamz. When Sheridan Rousseau walks into Lisette Mouton's charming little bookstore in Quebec City, she unknowingly holds the key to a mysterious box hidden in a secret room. (978-1-63679-900-1)

**Heart's Run** by D. Jackson Leigh. Hoping to recover an escaped racing mare, stock transporter Tobie Mason locks horns with local wild horse advocate Maggie Wilkes. (978-1-63679-825-7)

**Scandalous** by Kris Bryant. When a Hollywood actress trades places with her twin sister, everyone's in an uproar about getting duped, but Lindsay's more concerned about finding out which twin she made out with. (978-1-63679-874-5)

**The Art of Love** by Ali Vali. When Mimi and Bianca both set their sights on Jolly, sparks fly, loyalties are tested, and hearts collide as they navigate the unpredictable nature of their hearts (978-1-63679-719-9)

**The Other Side of Forever** by Kel McCord. Will Kenzie and Rachel be able to make love work when Rachel's cozy suburban dream feels like Kenzie's worst nightmare? (978-1-63679-812-7)

**The Secrets of Rhydian Hill** by Ronica Black. A doctor in need of a new start. A woman running from a killer. A love story that could end in tragedy. (978-1-63679-880-6)

**Feeling Lucky** by Krystina Rivers. What happens when, despite suddenly having enough money to buy almost anything, Lucy and Tanner start to discover that maybe all they need is each other? (978-1-63679-876-9)

**Iceberg** by Gun Brooke. When Lady Arabella hires Zandra, she never expects to find love, especially not as a disaster looms on the horizon. (978-1-63679-908-7)

**It Happened One Semester** by Aurora Rey. After a Pride night hookup, can eager new Assistant Professor Hudson Greene and Dean of Advising Callie Shaw overcome the odds and ace falling in love? (978-1-63679-814-1)

**It's Kind of a Bad Idea** by Sarah G. Levine. What happens when an emotionally unavailable serial dater meets the one woman she can't help but fall for—who happens to be the one woman who told her not to? (978-1-63679-920-9)

**Thankful for You** by Tagan Shepard. Everyone deserves to find their person, maybe Karen has finally found hers? (978-1-63679-884-4)

**What Happens on Location** by Nan Campbell. How can Helen produce a successful movie when its director is the woman responsible for the demise of her marriage? (978-1-63679-904-9)

**When Love Comes Around** by Radclyffe and Ronica Black. Can Maya Sanchez and Nolan Wright trust each other enough to build something real, or will the past tear them apart? (978-1-63679-930-8)

**Anywhere with You** by Margo Glynn. On a road trip through the Great American Southwest, two friends discover nature, hope, and each other. (978-1-63679-907-0)

**Burning Bridges** by Lesley Davis. Can Clancy and Jude crack the case of eight missing women—and the secrets of their own hearts? (978-1-63679-872-1)

**Dreams Entangled** by Sophia Kell Hagin. Amid self-doubt, secrets, a pandemic, fear of attack and attempted murder, Pirin and Gracie's attraction turns to love and their lives will never be the same. (978-1-63679-892-9)

**Echoes of Love** by Catherine Lane. As Hazel's and Jo's paths intertwine, they're swept up in a whirlwind of long-buried secrets, sizzling chemistry, and memories that won't be denied. (978-1-63679-835-6)

**Moonlight Obsession** by Sheri Lewis Wohl. All it takes to stop a clever killer is moonlight, love, and a silver bullet. (978-1-63679-831-8)

**My Boyfriend's Wife** by Joy Argento. Amid betrayal and heartbreak, can two women discover a love that could heal their pasts and rewrite their futures? (978-1-63679-866-0)

**Tapout** by Nicole Disney. A struggling MMA fighter finds her edge in an underground ring, but as she falls for the magnetic and ambitious promoter behind the matches, their dangerous world threatens to destroy everything they've fought to rebuild. (978-1-63679-924-7)

**The Fame Game** by Ronica Black. Wild child Hollywood actress Luna Kirkman begins dating Hollywood's leading man, only to fall for his straitlaced sister instead. (978-1-63679-858-5)

**An Extraordinary Passion** by Kit Meredith. An autistic podcaster must decide whether to take a chance on her polyamorous guest and indulge their shared passion, despite her history. (978-1-63679-679-6)

**That's Amore!** by Georgia Beers. The romantic city of Rome should inspire Lily's passion for writing, if she can look away from Marina Troiani, her witty, smart, and unassumingly beautiful Italian tour guide. (978-1-63679-841-7)

**The Unexpected Heiress** by Cassidy Crane. When a cynical opportunist meets a shy but spirited heiress, the last thing she plans is for her heart to get involved. (978-1-63679-833-2)

**Through Sky and Stars** by Tessa Croft. Can Val and Nicole's love cross space and time to change the fate of humanity? (978-1-63679-862-2)

**Uncomplicate It** by Kel McCord. When an office attraction threatens her career, Hollis Reed's carefully laid plans demand revision. (978-1-63679-864-6)

**Vanguard** by Gun Brooke. Beth Wild, Subterranean freedom fighter, is in the crosshairs when she fights for her people and risks her heart for loving the exacting Celestial dissident leader, LaSierra Delmonte. (978-1-63679-818-9)

**Wild Night Rising** by Barbara Ann Wright. Riding Harleys instead of horses, the Wild Hunt of myth is once again unleashed upon the world. Their ousted leader and a fey cop must join forces to rein in the ride of terror. (978-1-63679-749-6)